Joyce
Marx
Abbott Hardy Austen
Defoe Machiavelli Chesterton Emerson Hugo
Melville Montaigne Cooper Eliot Grimm
Haggard Molière
Stoker Christie Byron Schiller
Wilde Carroll Maupassant Engels
Garnett Fitzgerald Hawthorne Smith Kafka
Goethe Einstein Dostoyevsky Hall
Cotton Kipling Doyle Willis
Baum Henry Nietzsche
Leslie Dumas Flaubert Turgenev Balzac
Stockton Vatsyayana Crane
Burroughs Verne
Curtis Tocqueville Whitman Gogol Vinci
Homer Widger Tolstoy Busch
Darwin Thoreau Twain Scott
Potter Freud Zola Lawrence Plato Harte
Kant Jowett Stevenson Dickens
Andersen Burton Hesse
London Descartes Cervantes
Poe Aristotle Wells Voltaire
Hale James Hastings Cooke
Bunner Shakespeare Irving
Richter Chambers
Doré Dante Chekhov da Shaw Benedict Alcott
Swift Wodehouse Pushkin
Newton

 tredition®

tredition was established in 2006 by Sandra Latusseck and Soenke Schulz. Based in Hamburg, Germany, tredition offers publishing solutions to authors and publishing houses, combined with world-wide distribution of printed and digital book content. tredition is uniquely positioned to enable authors and publishing houses to create books on their own terms and without conventional manu-facturing risks.

For more information please visit: www.tredition.com

TREDITION CLASSICS

This book is part of the TREDITION CLASSICS series. The creators of this series are united by passion for literature and driven by the intention of making all public domain books available in printed format again - worldwide. Most TREDITION CLASSICS titles have been out of print and off the bookstore shelves for decades. At tredi-tion we believe that a great book never goes out of style and that its value is eternal. Several mostly non-profit literature projects pro-vide content to tredition. To support their good work, tredition donates a portion of the proceeds from each sold copy. As a reader of a TREDITION CLASSICS book, you support our mission to save many of the amazing works of world literature from oblivion. See all available books at www.tredition.com.

Project Gutenberg

The content for this book has been graciously provided by Project Gutenberg. Project Gutenberg is a non-profit organization founded by Michael Hart in 1971 at the University of Illinois. The mission of Project Gutenberg is simple: To encourage the creation and distribu-tion of eBooks. Project Gutenberg is the first and largest collection of public domain eBooks.

Memoirs of Carwin, the Biloquist

Charles Brockden Brown

Imprint

This book is part of TREDITION CLASSICS

Author: Charles Brockden Brown
Cover design: Buchgut, Berlin – Germany

Publisher: tredition GmbH, Hamburg - Germany
ISBN: 978-3-8424-2682-5

www.tredition.com
www.tredition.de

Copyright:
The content of this book is sourced from the public domain.

The intention of the TREDITION CLASSICS series is to make world literature in the public domain available in printed format. Literary enthusiasts and organizations, such as Project Gutenberg, worldwide have scanned and digitally edited the original texts. tredition has subsequently formatted and redesigned the content into a modern reading layout. Therefore, we cannot guarantee the exact reproduction of the original format of a particular historic edition. Please also note that no modifications have been made to the spelling, therefore it may differ from the orthography used today.

MEMOIRS OF CARWIN THE BILOQUIST

[A fragment]

By Charles Brockden Brown

[1803-1805]

Chapter I.

I was the second son of a farmer, whose place of residence was a western district of Pennsylvania. My eldest brother seemed fitted by nature for the employment to which he was destined. His wishes never led him astray from the hay-stack and the furrow. His ideas never ranged beyond the sphere of his vision, or suggested the possibility that to-morrow could differ from to-day. He could read and write, because he had no alternative between learning the lesson prescribed to him, and punishment. He was diligent, as long as fear urged him forward, but his exertions ceased with the cessation of this motive. The limits of his acquirements consisted in signing his name, and spelling out a chapter in the bible.

My character was the reverse of his. My thirst of knowledge was augmented in proportion as it was supplied with gratification. The more I heard or read, the more restless and unconquerable my curiosity became. My senses were perpetually alive to novelty, my fancy teemed with visions of the future, and my attention fastened upon every thing mysterious or unknown.

My father intended that my knowledge should keep pace with that of my brother, but conceived that all beyond the mere capacity to write and read was useless or pernicious. He took as much pains to keep me within these limits, as to make the acquisitions of my brother come up to them, but his efforts were not equally successful in both cases. The most vigilant and jealous scrutiny was exerted in vain: Reproaches and blows, painful privations and ignominious penances had no power to slacken my zeal and abate my perseverance. He might enjoin upon me the most laborious tasks, set the envy of my brother to watch me during the performance, make the most diligent search after my books, and destroy them without mercy, when they were found; but he could not outroot my darling propensity. I exerted all my powers to elude his watchfulness. Censures and stripes were sufficiently unpleasing to make me strive to avoid them. To effect this desirable end, I was incessantly employed in the invention of stratagems and the execution of expedients.

My passion was surely not deserving of blame, and I have frequently lamented the hardships to which it subjected me; yet, perhaps, the claims which were made upon my ingenuity and fortitude were not without beneficial effects upon my character.

This contention lasted from the sixth to the fourteenth year of my age. My father's opposition to my schemes was incited by a sincere though unenlightened desire for my happiness. That all his efforts were secretly eluded or obstinately repelled, was a source of the bitterest regret. He has often lamented, with tears, what he called my incorrigible depravity, and encouraged himself to perseverance by the notion of the ruin that would inevitably overtake me if I were allowed to persist in my present career. Perhaps the sufferings which arose to him from the disappointment, were equal to those which he inflicted on me.

In my fourteenth year, events happened which ascertained my future destiny. One evening I had been sent to bring cows from a meadow, some miles distant from my father's mansion. My time was limited, and I was menaced with severe chastisement if, according to my custom, I should stay beyond the period assigned.

For some time these menaces rung in my ears, and I went on my way with speed. I arrived at the meadow, but the cattle had broken the fence and escaped. It was my duty to carry home the earliest tidings of this accident, but the first suggestion was to examine the cause and manner of this escape. The field was bounded by cedar railing. Five of these rails were laid horizontally from post to post. The upper one had been broken in the middle, but the rest had merely been drawn out of the holes on one side, and rested with their ends on the ground. The means which had been used for this end, the reason why one only was broken, and that one the uppermost, how a pair of horns could be so managed as to effect that which the hands of man would have found difficult, supplied a theme of meditation.

Some accident recalled me from this reverie, and reminded me how much time had thus been consumed. I was terrified at the consequences of my delay, and sought with eagerness how they might be obviated. I asked myself if there were not a way back shorter than that by which I had come. The beaten road was rendered circuitous by a precipice that projected into a neighbouring stream, and closed up a passage by which the length of the way would have been diminished one half: at the foot of the cliff the water was of considerable depth, and agitated by an eddy. I could not estimate the danger which I should incur by plunging into it, but I was resolved to make the attempt. I have reason to think, that this experiment, if it had been tried, would have proved fatal, and my father, while he lamented my untimely fate, would have been wholly unconscious that his own unreasonable demands had occasioned it.

I turned my steps towards the spot. To reach the edge of the stream was by no means an easy undertaking, so many abrupt points and gloomy hollows were interposed. I had frequently skirted and penetrated this tract, but had never been so completely entangled in the maze as now: hence I had remained unacquainted with a narrow pass, which, at the distance of an hundred yards from the river, would conduct me, though not without danger and toil, to the opposite side of the ridge.

This glen was now discovered, and this discovery induced me to change my plan. If a passage could be here effected, it would be shorter and safer than that which led through the stream, and its practicability was to be known only by experiment. The path was narrow, steep, and overshadowed by rocks. The sun was nearly set, and the shadow of the cliff above, obscured the passage almost as much as midnight would have done: I was accustomed to despise danger when it presented itself in a sensible form, but, by a defect common in every one's education, goblins and spectres were to me the objects of the most violent apprehensions. These were unavoidably connected with solitude and darkness, and were present to my fears when I entered this gloomy recess.

These terrors are always lessened by calling the attention away to some indifferent object. I now made use of this expedient, and began to amuse myself by hallowing as loud as organs of unusual compass and vigour would enable me. I uttered the words which chanced to occur to me, and repeated in the shrill tones of a Mohock savage... "Cow! cow! come home! home!"... These notes were of course reverberated from the rocks which on either side towered aloft, but the echo was confused and indistinct.

I continued, for some time, thus to beguile the way, till I reached a space more than commonly abrupt, and which required all my attention. My rude ditty was suspended till I had surmounted this impediment. In a few minutes I was at leisure to renew it. After finishing the strain, I paused. In a few seconds a voice as I then imagined, uttered the same cry from the point of a rock some hundred feet behind me; the same words, with equal distinctness and deliberation, and in the same tone, appeared to be spoken. I was startled by this incident, and cast a fearful glance behind, to discover by whom it was uttered. The spot where I stood was buried in dusk, but the eminences were still invested with a luminous and vivid twilight. The speaker, however, was concealed from my view.

I had scarcely begun to wonder at this occurrence, when a new occasion for wonder, was afforded me. A few seconds, in like manner, elapsed, when my ditty was again rehearsed, with a no less perfect imitation, in a different quarter..... To this quarter I eagerly turned my eyes, but no one was visible.... The station, indeed, which this new speaker seemed to occupy, was inaccessible to man or beast.

If I were surprized at this second repetition of my words, judge how much my surprise must have been augmented, when the same calls were a third time repeated, and coming still in a new direction. Five times was this ditty successively resounded, at intervals nearly equal, always from a new quarter, and with little abatement of its original distinctness and force.

A little reflection was sufficient to shew that this was no more than an echo of an extraordinary kind. My terrors were quickly supplanted by delight. The motives to dispatch were forgotten, and I amused myself for an hour, with talking to these cliffs: I placed myself in new positions, and exhausted my lungs and my invention in new clamours.

The pleasures of this new discovery were an ample compensation for the ill treatment which I expected on my return. By some caprice in my father I escaped merely with a few reproaches. I seized the first opportunity of again visiting this recess, and repeating my amusement; time, and incessant repetition, could scarcely lessen its charms or exhaust the variety produced by new tones and new positions.

The hours in which I was most free from interruption and restraint were those of moonlight. My brother and I occupied a small room above the kitchen, disconnected, in some degree, with the rest of the house. It was the rural custom to retire early to bed and to anticipate the rising of the sun. When the moonlight was strong enough to permit me to read, it was my custom to escape from bed, and hie with my book to some neighbouring eminence, where I would remain stretched on the mossy rock, till the sinking or beclouded moon, forbade me to continue my employment. I was indebted for books to a friendly person in the neighbourhood, whose compliance with my solicitations was prompted partly by benevolence and partly by enmity to my father, whom he could not more egregiously offend than by gratifying my perverse and pernicious curiosity.

In leaving my chamber I was obliged to use the utmost caution to avoid rousing my brother, whose temper disposed him to thwart me in the least of my gratifications. My purpose was surely laudable, and yet on leaving the house and returning to it, I was obliged to use the vigilance and circumspection of a thief.

One night I left my bed with this view. I posted first to my vocal glen, and thence scrambling up a neighbouring steep, which overlooked a wide extent of this romantic country, gave myself up to contemplation, and the perusal of Milton's Comus.

My reflections were naturally suggested by the singularity of this echo. To hear my own voice speak at a distance would have been formerly regarded as prodigious. To hear too, that voice, not uttered by another, by whom it might easily be mimicked, but by myself! I cannot now recollect the transition which led me to the notion of sounds, similar to these, but produced by other means than reverberation. Could I not so dispose my organs as to make my voice appear at a distance?

From speculation I proceeded to experiment. The idea of a distant voice, like my own, was intimately present to my fancy. I exerted myself with a most ardent desire, and with something like a persuasion that I should succeed. I started with surprise, for it seemed as if success had crowned my attempts. I repeated the effort, but failed. A certain position of the organs took place on the first attempt, altogether new, unexampled and as it were, by accident, for I could not attain it on the second experiment.

You will not wonder that I exerted myself with indefatigable zeal to regain what had once, though for so short a space, been in my power. Your own ears have witnessed the success of these efforts. By perpetual exertion I gained it a second time, and now was a diligent observer of the circumstances attending it. Gradually I subjected these finer and more subtle motions to the command of my will. What was at first difficult, by exercise and habit, was rendered easy. I learned to accommodate my voice to all the varieties of distance and direction.

It cannot be denied that this faculty is wonderful and rare, but when we consider the possible modifications of muscular motion, how few of these are usually exerted, how imperfectly they are subjected to the will, and yet that the will is capable of being rendered unlimited and absolute, will not our wonder cease?

We have seen men who could hide their tongues so perfectly that even an Anatomist, after the most accurate inspection that a living subject could admit, has affirmed the organ to be wanting, but this was effected by the exertion of muscles unknown and incredible to the greater part of mankind.

The concurrence of teeth, palate and tongue, in the formation of speech should seem to be indispensable, and yet men have spoken distinctly though wanting a tongue, and to whom, therefore, teeth and palate were superfluous. The tribe of motions requisite to this end, are wholly latent and unknown, to those who possess that organ.

I mean not to be more explicit. I have no reason to suppose a peculiar conformation or activity in my own organs, or that the power which I possess may not, with suitable directions and by steady efforts, be obtained by others, but I will do nothing to facilitate the acquisition. It is by far, too liable to perversion for a good man to desire to possess it, or to teach it to another.

There remained but one thing to render this instrument as powerful in my hands as it was capable of being. From my childhood, I was remarkably skilful at imitation. There were few voices whether of men or birds or beasts which I could not imitate with success. To add my ancient, to my newly acquired skill, to talk from a distance, and at the same time, in the accents of another, was the object of my endeavours, and this object, after a certain number of trials, I finally obtained.

In my present situation every thing that denoted intellectual exertion was a crime, and exposed me to invectives if not to stripes. This circumstance induced me to be silent to all others, on the subject of my discovery. But, added to this, was a confused belief, that it might be made, in some way instrumental to my relief from the hardships and restraints of my present condition. For some time I was not aware of the mode in which it might be rendered subservient to this end.

Chapter II.

My father's sister was an ancient lady, resident in Philadelphia, the relict of a merchant, whose decease left her the enjoyment of a frugal competence. She was without children, and had often expressed her desire that her nephew Frank, whom she always considered as a sprightly and promising lad, should be put under her care. She offered to be at the expense of my education, and to bequeath to me at her death her slender patrimony.

This arrangement was obstinately rejected by my father, because it was merely fostering and giving scope to propensities, which he considered as hurtful, and because his avarice desired that this inheritance should fall to no one but himself. To me, it was a scheme of ravishing felicity, and to be debarred from it was a source of anguish known to few. I had too much experience of my father's pertinaciousness ever to hope for a change in his views; yet the bliss of living with my aunt, in a new and busy scene, and in the unbounded indulgence of my literary passion, continually occupied my thoughts: for a long time these thoughts were productive only of despondency and tears.

Time only enhanced the desirableness of this scheme; my new faculty would naturally connect itself with these wishes, and the question could not fail to occur whether it might not aid me in the execution of my favourite plan.

A thousand superstitious tales were current in the family. Apparitions had been seen, and voices had been heard on a multitude of occasions. My father was a confident believer in supernatural tokens. The voice of his wife, who had been many years dead, had been twice heard at midnight whispering at his pillow. I frequently asked myself whether a scheme favourable to my views might not be built upon these foundations. Suppose (thought I) my mother should be made to enjoin upon him compliance with my wishes?

This idea bred in me a temporary consternation. To imitate the voice of the dead, to counterfeit a commission from heaven, bore the aspect of presumption and impiety. It seemed an offence which could not fail to draw after it the vengeance of the deity. My wishes for a time yielded to my fears, but this scheme in proportion as I meditated on it, became more plausible; no other occurred to me so easy and so efficacious. I endeavoured to persuade myself that the end proposed, was, in the highest degree praiseworthy, and that the excellence of my purpose would justify the means employed to attain it.

My resolutions were, for a time, attended with fluctuations and misgivings. These gradually disappeared, and my purpose became firm; I was next to devise the means of effecting my views, this did not demand any tedious deliberation. It was easy to gain access to my father's chamber without notice or detection, cautious footsteps and the suppression of breath would place me, unsuspected and unthought of, by his bed side. The words I should use, and the mode of utterance were not easily settled, but having at length selected these, I made myself by much previous repetition, perfectly familiar with the use of them.

I selected a blustering and inclement night, in which the darkness was augmented by a veil of the blackest clouds. The building we inhabited was slight in its structure, and full of crevices through which the gale found easy way, and whistled in a thousand cadences. On this night the elemental music was remarkably sonorous, and was mingled not unfrequently with *thunder heard remote.*

I could not divest myself of secret dread. My heart faultered with a consciousness of wrong. Heaven seemed to be present and to disapprove my work; I listened to the thunder and the wind, as to the stern voice of this disapprobation. Big drops stood on my forehead, and my tremors almost incapacitated me from proceeding.

These impediments however I surmounted; I crept up stairs at midnight, and entered my father's chamber. The darkness was intense and I sought with outstretched hands for his bed. The darkness, added to the trepidation of my thoughts, disabled me from making a right estimate of distances: I was conscious of this, and when I advanced within the room, paused.

I endeavoured to compare the progress I had made with my knowledge of the room, and governed by the result of this comparison, proceeded cautiously and with hands still outstretched in search of the foot of the bed. At this moment lightning flashed into the room: the brightness of the gleam was dazzling, yet it afforded me an exact knowledge of my situation. I had mistaken my way, and discovered that my knees nearly touched the bedstead, and that my hands at the next step, would have touched my father's cheek. His closed eyes and every line in his countenance, were painted, as it were, for an instant on my sight.

The flash was accompanied with a burst of thunder, whose vehemence was stunning. I always entertained a dread of thunder, and now recoiled, overborne with terror. Never had I witnessed so luminous a gleam and so tremendous a shock, yet my father's slumber appeared not to be disturbed by it.

I stood irresolute and trembling; to prosecute my purpose in this state of mind was impossible. I resolved for the present to relinquish it, and turned with a view of exploring my way out of the chamber. Just then a light seen through the window, caught my eye. It was at first weak but speedily increased; no second thought was necessary to inform me that the barn, situated at a small distance from the house, and newly stored with hay, was in flames, in consequence of being struck by the lightning.

My terror at this spectacle made me careless of all consequences relative to myself. I rushed to the bed and throwing myself on my father, awakened him by loud cries. The family were speedily roused, and were compelled to remain impotent spectators of the devastation. Fortunately the wind blew in a contrary direction, so that our habitation was not injured.

The impression that was made upon me by the incidents of that night is indelible. The wind gradually rose into an hurricane; the largest branches were torn from the trees, and whirled aloft into the air; others were uprooted and laid prostrate on the ground. The barn was a spacious edifice, consisting wholly of wood, and filled with a plenteous harvest. Thus supplied with fuel, and fanned by the wind, the fire raged with incredible fury; meanwhile clouds rolled above, whose blackness was rendered more conspicuous by reflection from the flames; the vast volumes of smoke were dissipated in a moment by the storm, while glowing fragments and cinders were borne to an immense hight, and tossed everywhere in wild confusion. Ever and anon the sable canopy that hung around us was streaked with lightning, and the peals, by which it was accompanied, were deafning, and with scarcely any intermission.

It was, doubtless, absurd to imagine any connexion between this portentous scene and the purpose that I had meditated, yet a belief of this connexion, though wavering and obscure, lurked in my mind; something more than a coincidence merely casual, appeared to have subsisted between my situation, at my father's bed side, and the flash that darted through the window, and diverted me from my design. It palsied my courage, and strengthened my conviction, that my scheme was criminal.

After some time had elapsed, and tranquility was, in some degree, restored in the family, my father reverted to the circumstances in which I had been discovered on the first alarm of this event. The truth was impossible to be told. I felt the utmost reluctance to be guilty of a falsehood, but by falsehood only could I elude detection. That my guilt was the offspring of a fatal necessity, that the injustice of others gave it birth and made it unavoidable, afforded me slight consolation. Nothing can be more injurious than a lie, but its evil tendency chiefly respects our future conduct. Its direct consequences may be transient and few, but it facilitates a repetition, strengthens temptation, and grows into habit. I pretended some necessity had drawn me from my bed, and that discovering the condition of the barn, I hastened to inform my father.

Some time after this, my father summoned me to his presence. I had been previously guilty of disobedience to his commands, in a matter about which he was usually very scrupulous. My brother had been privy to my offence, and had threatened to be my accuser. On this occasion I expected nothing but arraignment and punishment. Weary of oppression, and hopeless of any change in my father's temper and views, I had formed the resolution of eloping from his house, and of trusting, young as I was, to the caprice of fortune. I was hesitating whether to abscond without the knowledge of the family, or to make my resolutions known to them, and while I avowed my resolution, to adhere to it in spite of opposition and remonstrances, when I received this summons.

I was employed at this time in the field; night was approaching, and I had made no preparation for departure; all the preparation in my power to make, was indeed small; a few clothes, made into a bundle, was the sum of my possessions. Time would have little influence in improving my prospects, and I resolved to execute my scheme immediately.

I left my work intending to seek my chamber, and taking what was my own, to disappear forever. I turned a stile that led out of the field into a bye path, when my father appeared before me, advancing in an opposite direction; to avoid him was impossible, and I summoned my fortitude to a conflict with his passion.

As soon as we met, instead of anger and upbraiding, he told me, that he had been reflecting on my aunt's proposal, to take me under her protection, and had concluded that the plan was proper; if I still retained my wishes on that head, he would readily comply with them, and that, if I chose, I might set off for the city next morning, as a neighbours waggon was preparing to go.

I shall not dwell on the rapture with which this proposal was listened to: it was with difficulty that I persuaded myself that he was in earnest in making it, nor could divine the reasons, for so sudden and unexpected a change in his maxims.... These I afterwards discovered. Some one had instilled into him fears, that my aunt exasperated at his opposition to her request, respecting the unfortunate Frank, would bequeath her property to strangers; to obviate this evil, which his avarice prompted him to regard as much greater than any mischief, that would accrue to me, from the change of my abode, he embraced her proposal.

I entered with exultation and triumph on this new scene; my hopes were by no means disappointed. Detested labour was exchanged for luxurious idleness. I was master of my time, and the chuser of my occupations. My kinswoman on discovering that I entertained no relish for the drudgery of colleges, and was contented with the means of intellectual gratification, which I could obtain under her roof, allowed me to pursue my own choice.

Three tranquil years passed away, during which, each day added to my happiness, by adding to my knowledge. My biloquial faculty was not neglected. I improved it by assiduous exercise; I deeply reflected on the use to which it might be applied. I was not destitute of pure intentions; I delighted not in evil; I was incapable of knowingly contributing to another's misery, but the sole or principal end of my endeavours was not the happiness of others.

I was actuated by ambition. I was delighted to possess superior power; I was prone to manifest that superiority, and was satisfied if this were done, without much solicitude concerning consequences. I sported frequently with the apprehensions of my associates, and threw out a bait for their wonder, and supplied them with occasions for the structure of theories. It may not be amiss to enumerate one or two adventures in which I was engaged.

Chapter III.

I had taken much pains to improve the sagacity of a favourite Spaniel. It was my purpose, indeed, to ascertain to what degree of improvement the principles of reasoning and imitation could be carried in a dog. There is no doubt that the animal affixes distinct ideas to sounds. What are the possible limits of his vocabulary no one can tell. In conversing with my dog I did not use English words, but selected simple monosyllables. Habit likewise enabled him to comprehend my gestures. If I crossed my hands on my breast he understood the signal and laid down behind me. If I joined my hands and lifted them to my breast, he returned home. If I grasped one arm above the elbow he ran before me. If I lifted my hand to my forehead he trotted composedly behind. By one motion I could make him bark; by another I could reduce him to silence. He would howl in twenty different strains of mournfulness, at my bidding. He would fetch and carry with undeviating faithfulness.

His actions being thus chiefly regulated by gestures, that to a stranger would appear indifferent or casual, it was easy to produce a belief that the animal's knowledge was much greater than in truth, it was.

One day, in a mixed company, the discourse turned upon the un-rivaled abilities of *Damon*. Damon had, indeed, acquired in all the circles which I frequented, an extraordinary reputation. Numerous instances of his sagacity were quoted and some of them exhibited on the spot. Much surprise was excited by the readiness with which he appeared to comprehend sentences of considerable abstraction and complexity, though, he in reality, attended to nothing but the movements of hand or fingers with which I accompanied my words. I enhanced the astonishment of some and excited the ridicule of others, by observing that my dog not only understood English when spoken by others, but actually spoke the language himself, with no small degree of precision.

This assertion could not be admitted without proof; proof, therefore, was readily produced. At a known signal, Damon began a low interrupted noise, in which the astonished hearers clearly distinguished English words. A dialogue began between the animal and his master, which was maintained, on the part of the former, with great vivacity and spirit. In this dialogue the dog asserted the dignity of his species and capacity of intellectual improvement. The company separated lost in wonder, but perfectly convinced by the evidence that had been produced.

On a subsequent occasion a select company was assembled at a garden, at a small distance from the city. Discourse glided through a variety of topics, till it lighted at length on the subject of invisible beings. From the speculations of philosophers we proceeded to the creations of the poet. Some maintained the justness of Shakspear's delineations of aerial beings, while others denied it. By no violent transition, Ariel and his songs were introduced, and a lady, celebrated for her musical skill, was solicited to accompany her pedal harp with the song of "Five fathom deep thy father lies"... She was known to have set, for her favourite instrument, all the songs of Shakspeare.

My youth made me little more than an auditor on this occasion. I sat apart from the rest of the company, and carefully noted every thing. The track which the conversation had taken, suggested a scheme which was not thoroughly digested when the lady began her enchanting strain.

She ended and the audience were mute with rapture. The pause continued, when a strain was wafted to our ears from another quarter. The spot where we sat was embowered by a vine. The verdant arch was lofty and the area beneath was spacious.

The sound proceeded from above. At first it was faint and scarcely audible; presently it reached a louder key, and every eye was cast up in expectation of beholding a face among the pendant clusters. The strain was easily recognized, for it was no other than that which Ariel is made to sing when finally absolved from the service of the wizard.

> In the Cowslips bell I lie, On the Bat's back I do fly... After summer merrily, &c.

Their hearts palpitated as they listened: they gazed at each other for a solution of the mystery. At length the strain died away at distance, and an interval of silence was succeded by an earnest discussion of the cause of this prodigy. One supposition only could be adopted, which was, that the strain was uttered by human organs. That the songster was stationed on the roof of the arbour, and having finished his melody had risen into the viewless fields of air.

I had been invited to spend a week at this house: this period was nearly expired when I received information that my aunt was suddenly taken sick, and that her life was in imminent danger. I immediately set out on my return to the city, but before my arrival she was dead.

This lady was entitled to my gratitude and esteem; I had received the most essential benefits at her hand. I was not destitute of sensibility, and was deeply affected by this event: I will own, however, that my grief was lessened by reflecting on the consequences of her death, with regard to my own condition. I had been ever taught to consider myself as her heir, and her death, therefore, would free me from certain restraints.

My aunt had a female servant, who had lived with her for twenty years: she was married, but her husband, who was an artizan, lived apart from her: I had no reason to suspect the woman's sincerity and disinterestedness; but my aunt was no sooner consigned to the grave than a will was produced, in which Dorothy was named her sole and universal heir.

It was in vain to urge my expectations and my claims.... the instrument was legibly and legally drawn up.... Dorothy was exasperated by my opposition and surmises, and vigorously enforced her title. In a week after the decease of my kinswoman, I was obliged to seek a new dwelling. As all my property consisted in my cloths and my papers, this was easily done.

My condition was now calamitous and forlorn. Confiding in the acquisition of my aunt's patrimony, I had made no other provision for the future; I hated manual labour, or any task of which the object was gain. To be guided in my choice of occupations by any motive but the pleasure which the occupation was qualified to produce, was intolerable to my proud, indolent, and restive temper.

This resource was now cut off; the means of immediate subsistence were denied me: If I had determined to acquire the knowledge of some lucrative art, the acquisition would demand time, and, meanwhile, I was absolutely destitute of support. My father's house was, indeed, open to me, but I preferred to stifle myself with the filth of the kennel, rather than to return to it.

Some plan it was immediately necessary to adopt. The exigence of my affairs, and this reverse of fortune, continually occupied my thoughts; I estranged myself from society and from books, and devoted myself to lonely walks and mournful meditation.

One morning as I ranged along the bank of Schuylkill, I encountered a person, by name Ludloe, of whom I had some previous knowledge. He was from Ireland; was a man of some rank and apparently rich: I had met with him before, but in mixed companies, where little direct intercourse had taken place between us. Our last meeting was in the arbour where Ariel was so unexpectedly introduced.

Our acquaintance merely justified a transient salutation; but he did not content himself with noticing me as I passed, but joined me in my walk and entered into conversation. It was easy to advert to the occasion on which we had last met, and to the mysterious incident which then occurred. I was solicitous to dive into his thoughts upon this head and put some questions which tended to the point that I wished.

I was somewhat startled when he expressed his belief, that the performer of this mystic strain was one of the company then present, who exerted, for this end, a faculty not commonly possessed. Who this person was he did not venture to guess, and could not discover, by the tokens which he suffered to appear, that his suspicions glanced at me. He expatiated with great profoundness and fertility of ideas, on the uses to which a faculty like this might be employed. No more powerful engine, he said, could be conceived, by which the ignorant and credulous might be moulded to our purposes; managed by a man of ordinary talents, it would open for him the straightest and surest avenues to wealth and power.

His remarks excited in my mind a new strain of thoughts. I had not hitherto considered the subject in this light, though vague ideas of the importance of this art could not fail to be occasionally suggested: I ventured to inquire into his ideas of the mode, in which an art like this could be employed, so as to effect the purposes he mentioned.

He dealt chiefly in general representations. Men, he said, believed in the existence and energy of invisible powers, and in the duty of discovering and conforming to their will. This will was supposed to be sometimes made known to them through the medium of their senses. A voice coming from a quarter where no attendant form could be seen would, in most cases, be ascribed to supernal agency, and a command imposed on them, in this manner, would be obeyed with religious scrupulousness. Thus men might be imperiously directed in the disposal of their industry, their property, and even of their lives. Men, actuated by a mistaken sense of duty, might, under this influence, be led to the commission of the most flagitious, as well as the most heroic acts: If it were his desire to accumulate wealth, or institute a new sect, he should need no other instrument.

I listened to this kind of discourse with great avidity, and regretted when he thought proper to introduce new topics. He ended by requesting me to visit him, which I eagerly consented to do. When left alone, my imagination was filled with the images suggested by this conversation. The hopelessness of better fortune, which I had lately harboured, now gave place to cheering confidence. Those motives of rectitude which should deter me from this species of imposture, had never been vivid or stable, and were still more weakened by the artifices of which I had already been guilty. The utility or harmlessness of the end, justified, in my eyes, the means.

No event had been more unexpected, by me, than the bequest of my aunt to her servant. The will, under which the latter claimed, was dated prior to my coming to the city. I was not surprised, therefore, that it had once been made, but merely that it had never been cancelled or superseded by a later instrument. My wishes inclined me to suspect the existence of a later will, but I had conceived that, to ascertain its existence, was beyond my power.

Now, however, a different opinion began to be entertained. This woman like those of her sex and class was unlettered and superstitious. Her faith in spells and apparitions, was of the most lively kind. Could not her conscience be awakened by a voice from the grave! Lonely and at midnight, my aunt might be introduced, upbraiding her for her injustice, and commanding her to attone for it by acknowledging the claim of the rightful proprietor.

True it was, that no subsequent will might exist, but this was the fruit of mistake, or of negligence. She probably intended to cancel the old one, but this act might, by her own weakness, or by the artifices of her servant, be delayed till death had put it out of her power. In either case a mandate from the dead could scarcely fail of being obeyed.

I considered this woman as the usurper of my property. Her husband as well as herself, were laborious and covetous; their good fortune had made no change in their mode of living, but they were as frugal and as eager to accumulate as ever. In their hands, money was inert and sterile, or it served to foster their vices. To take it from them would, therefore, be a benefit both to them and to myself; not even an imaginary injury would be inflicted. Restitution, if legally compelled to it, would be reluctant and painful, but if enjoined by Heaven would be voluntary, and the performance of a seeming duty would carry with it, its own reward.

These reasonings, aided by inclination, were sufficient to determine me. I have no doubt but their fallacy would have been detected in the sequel, and my scheme have been productive of nothing but confusion and remorse. From these consequences, however, my fate interposed, as in the former instance, to save me.

Having formed my resolution, many preliminaries to its execution were necessary to be settled. These demanded deliberation and delay; meanwhile I recollected my promise to Ludlow, and paid him a visit. I met a frank and affectionate reception. It would not be easy to paint the delight which I experienced in this man's society. I was at first oppressed with the sense of my own inferiority in age, knowledge and rank. Hence arose numberless reserves and incapacitating diffidences; but these were speedily dissipated by the fascinations of this man's address. His superiority was only rendered, by time, more conspicuous, but this superiority, by appearing never to be present to his own mind, ceased to be uneasy to me. My questions required to be frequently answered, and my mistakes to be rectified; but my keenest scrutiny, could detect in his manner, neither arrogance nor contempt. He seemed to talk merely from the overflow of his ideas, or a benevolent desire of imparting information.

Chapter IV.

My visits gradually became more frequent. Meanwhile my wants increased, and the necessity of some change in my condition became daily more urgent. This incited my reflections on the scheme which I had formed. The time and place suitable to my design, were not selected without much anxious inquiry and frequent waverings of purpose. These being at length fixed, the interval to elapse, before the carrying of my design into effect, was not without perturbation and suspense. These could not be concealed from my new friend and at length prompted him to inquire into the cause.

It was not possible to communicate the whole truth; but the warmth of his manner inspired me with some degree of ingenuousness. I did not hide from him my former hopes and my present destitute condition. He listened to my tale with no expressions of sympathy, and when I had finished, abruptly inquired whether I had any objection to a voyage to Europe? I answered in the negative. He then said that he was preparing to depart in a fortnight and advised me to make up my mind to accompany him.

This unexpected proposal gave me pleasure and surprize, but the want of money occurred to me as an insuperable objection. On this being mentioned, Oho! said he, carelessly, that objection is easily removed, I will bear all expenses of your passage myself.

The extraordinary beneficence of this act as well as the air of uncautiousness attending it, made me doubt the sincerity of his offer, and when new declarations removed this doubt, I could not forbear expressing at once my sense of his generosity and of my own unworthiness.

He replied that generosity had been expunged from his catalogue as having no meaning or a vicious one. It was the scope of his exertions to be just. This was the sum of human duty, and he that fell short, ran beside, or outstripped justice was a criminal. What he gave me was my due or not my due. If it were my due, I might reasonably demand it from him and it was wicked to withhold it. Merit on one side or gratitude on the other, were contradictory and unintelligible.

If I were fully convinced that this benefit was not my due and yet received it, he should hold me in contempt. The rectitude of my principles and conduct would be the measure of his approbation, and no benefit should he ever bestow which the receiver was not entitled to claim, and which it would not be criminal in him to refuse.

These principles were not new from the mouth of Ludloe, but they had, hitherto, been regarded as the fruits of a venturous speculation in my mind. I had never traced them into their practical consequences, and if his conduct on this occasion had not squared with his maxims, I should not have imputed to him inconsistency. I did not ponder on these reasonings at this time: objects of immediate importance engrossed my thoughts.

One obstacle to this measure was removed. When my voyage was performed how should I subsist in my new abode? I concealed not my perplexity and he commented on it in his usual manner. How did I mean to subsist, he asked, in my own country? The means of living would be, at least, as much within my reach there as here. As to the pressure of immediate and absolute want, he believed I should be exposed to little hazard. With talents such as mine, I must be hunted by a destiny peculiarly malignant, if I could not provide myself with necessaries wherever my lot were cast.

He would make allowances, however, for my diffidence and self-distrust, and would obviate my fears by expressing his own intentions with regard to me. I must be apprized, however, of his true meaning. He laboured to shun all hurtful and vitious things, and therefore carefully abstained from making or confiding *in promises.* It was just to assist me in this voyage, and it would probably be equally just to continue to me similar assistance when it was finished. That indeed was a subject, in a great degree, within my own cognizance. His aid would be proportioned to my wants and to my merits, and I had only to take care that my claims were just, for them to be admitted.

This scheme could not but appear to me eligible. I thirsted after an acquaintance with new scenes; my present situation could not be changed for a worse; I trusted to the constancy of Ludloe's friendship; to this at least it was better to trust than to the success of my imposture on Dorothy, which was adopted merely as a desperate expedient: finally I determined to embark with him.

In the course of this voyage my mind was busily employed. There were no other passengers beside ourselves, so that my own condition and the character of Ludloe, continually presented themselves to my reflections. It will be supposed that I was not a vague or indifferent observer.

There were no vicissitudes in the deportment or lapses in the discourse of my friend. His feelings appeared to preserve an unchangeable tenor, and his thoughts and words always to flow with the same rapidity. His slumber was profound and his wakeful hours serene. He was regular and temperate in all his exercises and gratifications. Hence were derived his clear perceptions and exuberant health.

This treatment of me, like all his other mental and corporal operations, was modelled by one inflexible standard. Certain scruples and delicacies were incident to my situation. Of the existence of these he seemed to be unconscious, and yet nothing escaped him inconsistent with a state of absolute equality.

I was naturally inquisitive as to his fortune and the collateral circumstances of his condition. My notions of politeness hindered me from making direct inquiries. By indirect means I could gather nothing but that his state was opulent and independent, and that he had two sisters whose situation resembled his own.

Though, in conversation, he appeared to be governed by the utmost candour; no light was let in upon the former transactions of his life. The purpose of his visit to America I could merely guess to be the gratification of curiosity.

My future pursuits must be supposed chiefly to occupy my attention. On this head I was destitute of all stedfast views. Without profession or habits of industry or sources of permanent revenue, the world appeared to me an ocean on which my bark was set afloat, without compass or sail. The world into which I was about to enter, was untried and unknown, and though I could consent to profit by the guidance I was unwilling to rely on the support of others.

This topic being nearest my heart, I frequently introduced into conversation with my friend; but on this subject he always allowed himself to be led by me, while on all others, he was zealous to point the way. To every scheme that I proposed he was sure to cause objections. All the liberal professions were censured as perverting the understanding, by giving scope to the sordid motive of gain, or embuing the mind with erroneous principles. Skill was slowly obtained, and success, though integrity and independence must be given for it, dubious and instable. The mechanical trades were equally obnoxious; they were vitious by contributing to the spurious gratifications of the rich and multiplying the objects of luxury; they were destruction to the intellect and vigor of the artizan; they enervated his frame and brutalized his mind.

When I pointed out to him the necessity of some species of labour, he tacitly admitted that necessity, but refused to direct me in the choice of a pursuit, which though not free from defect should yet have the fewest inconveniences. He dwelt on the fewness of our actual wants, the temptations which attend the possession of wealth, the benefits of seclusion and privacy, and the duty of unfettering our minds from the prejudices which govern the world.

His discourse tended merely to unsettle my views and increase my perplexity. This effect was so uniform that I at length desisted from all allusions to this theme and endeavoured to divert my own reflections from it. When our voyage should be finished, and I should actually tread this new stage, I believed that I should be better qualified to judge of the measures to be taken by me.

At length we reached Belfast. From thence we immediately repaired to Dublin. I was admitted as a member of his family. When I expressed my uncertainty as to the place to which it would be proper for me to repair, he gave me a blunt but cordial invitation to his house. My circumstances allowed me no option and I readily complied. My attention was for a time engrossed by a diversified succession of new objects. Their novelty however disappearing, left me at liberty to turn my eyes upon myself and my companion, and here my reflections were supplied with abundant food.

His house was spacious and commodious, and furnished with profusion and elegance. A suit of apartments was assigned to me, in which I was permitted to reign uncontroled and access was permitted to a well furnished library. My food was furnished in my own room, prepared in the manner which I had previously directed. Occasionally Ludloe would request my company to breakfast, when an hour was usually consumed in earnest or sprightly conversation. At all other times he was invisible, and his apartments, being wholly separate from mine, I had no opportunity of discovering in what way his hours were employed.

He defended this mode of living as being most compatible with liberty. He delighted to expatiate on the evils of cohabitation. Men, subjected to the same regimen, compelled to eat and sleep and associate at certain hours, were strangers to all rational independence and liberty. Society would never be exempt from servitude and misery, till those artificial ties which held human beings together under the same roof were dissolved. He endeavoured to regulate his own conduct in pursuance of these principles, and to secure to himself as much freedom as the present regulations of society would permit. The same independence which he claimed for himself he likewise extended to me. The distribution of my own time, the selection of my own occupations and companions should belong to myself.

But these privileges, though while listening to his arguments I could not deny them to be valuable, I would have willingly dispensed with. The solitude in which I lived became daily more painful. I ate and drank, enjoyed clothing and shelter, without the exercise of forethought or industry; I walked and sat, went out and returned for as long and at what seasons I thought proper, yet my condition was a fertile source of discontent.

I felt myself removed to a comfortless and chilling distance from Ludloe. I wanted to share in his occupations and views. With all his ingenuousness of aspect and overflow of thoughts, when he allowed me his company, I felt myself painfully bewildered with regard to his genuine condition and sentiments.

He had it in his power to introduce me to society, and without an introduction, it was scarcely possible to gain access to any social circle or domestic fireside. Add to this, my own obscure prospects and dubious situation. Some regular intellectual pursuit would render my state less irksome, but I had hitherto adopted no scheme of this kind.

Chapter V.

Time tended, in no degree, to alleviate my dissatisfaction. It increased till the determination became at length formed of opening my thoughts to Ludloe. At the next breakfast interview which took place, I introduced the subject, and expatiated without reserve, on the state of my feelings. I concluded with entreating him to point out some path in which my talents might be rendered useful to himself or to mankind.

After a pause of some minutes, he said, What would you do? You forget the immaturity of your age. If you are qualified to act a part in the theatre of life, step forth; but you are not qualified. You want knowledge, and with this you ought previously to endow yourself..... Means, for this end, are within your reach. Why should you waste your time in idleness, and torment yourself with unprofitable wishes? Books are at hand.... books from which most sciences and languages can be learned. Read, analise, digest; collect facts, and investigate theories: ascertain the dictates of reason, and supply yourself with the inclination and the power to adhere to them. You will not, legally speaking, be a man in less than three years. Let this period be devoted to the acquisition of wisdom. Either stay here, or retire to an house I have on the banks of Killarney, where you will find all the conveniences of study.

I could not but reflect with wonder at this man's treatment of me. I could plead none of the rights of relationship; yet I enjoyed the privileges of a son. He had not imparted to me any scheme, by pursuit of which I might finally compensate him for the expense to which my maintenance and education would subject him. He gave me reason to hope for the continuance of his bounty. He talked and acted as if my fortune were totally disjoined from his; yet was I indebted to him for the morsel which sustained my life. Now it was proposed to withdraw myself to studious leisure, and romantic solitude. All my wants, personal and intellectual, were to be supplied gratuitously and copiously. No means were prescribed by which I might make compensation for all these benefits. In conferring them he seemed to be actuated by no view to his own ultimate advantage. He took no measures to secure my future services.

I suffered these thoughts to escape me, on this occasion, and observed that to make my application successful, or useful, it was necessary to pursue some end. I must look forward to some post which I might hereafter occupy beneficially to myself or others; and for which all the efforts of my mind should be bent to qualify myself.

These hints gave him visible pleasure; and now, for the first time, he deigned to advise me on this head. His scheme, however, was not suddenly produced. The way to it was circuitous and long. It was his business to make every new step appear to be suggested by my own reflections. His own ideas were the seeming result of the moment, and sprung out of the last idea that was uttered. Being hastily taken up, they were, of course, liable to objection. These objections, sometimes occurring to me and sometimes to him, were admitted or contested with the utmost candour. One scheme went through numerous modifications before it was proved to be ineligible, or before it yielded place to a better. It was easy to perceive, that books alone were insufficient to impart knowledge: that man must be examined with our own eyes to make us acquainted with their nature: that ideas collected from observation and reading, must correct and illustrate each other: that the value of all principles, and their truth, lie in their practical effects. Hence, gradually arose, the usefulness of travelling, of inspecting the habits and manners of a nation, and investigating, on the spot, the causes of their happiness and misery. Finally, it was determined that Spain was more suitable than any other, to the views of a judicious traveller.

My language, habits, and religion were mentioned as obstacles to close and extensive views; but these difficulties successively and slowly vanished. Converse with books, and natives of Spain, a steadfast purpose and unwearied diligence would efface all differences between me and a Castilian with respect to speech. Personal habits, were changeable, by the same means. The bars to unbounded intercourse, rising from the religion of Spain being irreconcilably opposite to mine, cost us no little trouble to surmount, and here the skill of Ludloe was eminently displayed.

I had been accustomed to regard as unquestionable, the fallacy of the Romish faith. This persuasion was habitual and the child of prejudice, and was easily shaken by the artifices of this logician. I was first led to bestow a kind of assent on the doctrines of the Roman church; but my convictions were easily subdued by a new species of argumentation, and, in a short time, I reverted to my ancient disbelief, so that, if an exterior conformity to the rights of Spain were requisite to the attainment of my purpose, that conformity must be dissembled.

My moral principles had hitherto been vague and unsettled. My circumstances had led me to the frequent practice of insincerity; but my transgressions as they were slight and transient, did not much excite my previous reflections, or subsequent remorse. My deviations, however, though rendered easy by habit, were by no means sanctioned by my principles. Now an imposture, more profound and deliberate, was projected; and I could not hope to perform well my part, unless steadfastly and thoroughly persuaded of its rectitude.

My friend was the eulogist of sincerity. He delighted to trace its influence on the happiness of mankind; and proved that nothing but the universal practice of this virtue was necessary to the perfection of human society. His doctrine was splendid and beautiful. To detect its imperfections was no easy task; to lay the foundations of virtue in utility, and to limit, by that scale, the operation of general principles; to see that the value of sincerity, like that of every other mode of action, consisted in its tendency to good, and that, therefore the obligation to speak truth was not paramount or intrinsical: that my duty is modelled on a knowledge and foresight of the conduct of others; and that, since men in their actual state, are infirm and deceitful, a just estimate of consequences may sometimes make dissimulation my duty were truths that did not speedily occur. The discovery, when made, appeared to be a joint work. I saw nothing in Ludlow but proofs of candour, and a judgment incapable of bias.

The means which this man employed to fit me for his purpose, perhaps owed their success to my youth and ignorance. I may have given you exaggerated ideas of his dexterity and address. Of that I am unable to judge. Certain it is, that no time or reflection has abated my astonishment at the profoundness of his schemes, and the perseverance with which they were pursued by him. To detail their progress would expose me to the risk of being tedious, yet none but minute details would sufficiently display his patience and subtlety.

It will suffice to relate, that after a sufficient period of preparation and arrangements being made for maintaining a copious intercourse with Ludlow, I embarked for Barcelona. A restless curiosity and vigorous application have distinguished my character in every scene. Here was spacious field for the exercise of all my energies. I sought out a preceptor in my new religion. I entered into the hearts of priests and confessors, the *hidalgo* and the peasant, the monk and the prelate, the austere and voluptuous devotee were scrutinized in all their forms.

Man was the chief subject of my study, and the social sphere that in which I principally moved; but I was not inattentive to inanimate nature, nor unmindful of the past. If the scope of virtue were to maintain the body in health, and to furnish its highest enjoyments to every sense, to increase the number, and accuracy, and order of our intellectual stores, no virtue was ever more unblemished than mine. If to act upon our conceptions of right, and to acquit ourselves of all prejudice and selfishness in the formation of our principles, entitle us to the testimony of a good conscience, I might justly claim it.

I shall not pretend to ascertain my rank in the moral scale. Your notions of duty differ widely from mine. If a system of deceit, pursued merely from the love of truth; if voluptuousness, never gratified at the expense of health, may incur censure, I am censurable. This, indeed, was not the limit of my deviations. Deception was often unnecessarily practised, and my biloquial faculty did not lie unemployed. What has happened to yourselves may enable you, in some degree, to judge of the scenes in which my mystical exploits engaged me. In none of them, indeed, were the effects equally disastrous, and they were, for the most part, the result of well digested projects.

To recount these would be an endless task. They were designed as mere specimens of power, to illustrate the influence of superstition: to give sceptics the consolation of certainty: to annihilate the scruples of a tender female, or facilitate my access to the bosoms of courtiers and monks.

The first achievement of this kind took place in the convent of the Escurial. For some time the hospitality of this brotherhood allowed me a cell in that magnificent and gloomy fabric. I was drawn hither chiefly by the treasures of Arabian literature, which are preserved here in the keeping of a learned Maronite, from Lebanon. Standing one evening on the steps of the great altar, this devout friar expatiated on the miraculous evidences of his religion; and, in a moment of enthusiasm, appealed to San Lorenzo, whose martyrdom was displayed before us. No sooner was the appeal made than the saint, obsequious to the summons, whispered his responses from the shrine, and commanded the heretic to tremble and believe. This event was reported to the convent. With whatever reluctance, I could not refuse my testimony to its truth, and its influence on my faith was clearly shewn in my subsequent conduct.

A lady of rank, in Seville, who had been guilty of many unauthorized indulgences, was, at last, awakened to remorse, by a voice from Heaven, which she imagined had commanded her to expiate her sins by an abstinence from all food for thirty days. Her friends found it impossible to outroot this persuasion, or to overcome her resolution even by force. I chanced to be one in a numerous company where she was present. This fatal illusion was mentioned, and an opportunity afforded to the lady of defending her scheme. At a pause in the discourse, a voice was heard from the ceiling, which confirmed the truth of her tale; but, at the same time revoked the command, and, in consideration of her faith, pronounced her absolution. Satisfied with this proof, the auditors dismissed their unbelief, and the lady consented to eat.

In the course of a copious correspondence with Ludlow, the observations I had collected were given. A sentiment, which I can hardly describe, induced me to be silent on all adventures connected with my bivocal projects. On other topics, I wrote fully, and without restraint. I painted, in vivid hues, the scenes with which I was daily conversant, and pursued, fearlessly, every speculation on religion and government that occurred. This spirit was encouraged by Ludloe, who failed not to comment on my narrative, and multiply deductions from my principles.

He taught me to ascribe the evils that infest society to the errors of opinion. The absurd and unequal distribution of power and property gave birth to poverty and riches, and these were the sources of luxury and crimes. These positions were readily admitted; but the remedy for these ills, the means of rectifying these errors were not easily discovered. We have been inclined to impute them to inherent defects in the moral constitution of men: that oppression and tyranny grow up by a sort of natural necessity, and that they will perish only when the human species is extinct. Ludloe laboured to prove that this was, by no means, the case: that man is the creature of circumstances: that he is capable of endless improvement: that his progress has been stopped by the artificial impediment of government: that by the removal of this, the fondest dreams of imagination will be realized.

From detailing and accounting for the evils which exist under our present institutions, he usually proceeded to delineate some scheme of Utopian felicity, where the empire of reason should supplant that of force: where justice should be universally understood and practised; where the interest of the whole and of the individual should be seen by all to be the same; where the public good should be the scope of all activity; where the tasks of all should be the same, and the means of subsistence equally distributed.

No one could contemplate his pictures without rapture. By their comprehensiveness and amplitude they filled the imagination. I was unwilling to believe that in no region of the world, or at no period could these ideas be realized. It was plain that the nations of Europe were tending to greater depravity, and would be the prey of perpetual vicissitude. All individual attempts at their reformation would be fruitless. He therefore who desired the diffusion of right principles, to make a just system be adopted by a whole community, must pursue some extraordinary method.

In this state of mind I recollected my native country, where a few colonists from Britain had sown the germe of populous and mighty empires. Attended, as they were, into their new abode, by all their prejudices, yet such had been the influence of new circumstances, of consulting for their own happiness, of adopting simple forms of government, and excluding nobles and kings from their system, that they enjoyed a degree of happiness far superior to their parent state.

To conquer the prejudices and change the habits of millions, are impossible. The human mind, exposed to social influences, inflexibly adheres to the direction that is given to it; but for the same reason why men, who begin in error will continue, those who commence in truth, may be expected to persist. Habit and example will operate with equal force in both instances.

Let a few, sufficiently enlightened and disinterested, take up their abode in some unvisited region. Let their social scheme be founded in equity, and how small soever their original number may be, their growth into a nation is inevitable. Among other effects of national justice, was to be ranked the swift increase of numbers. Exempt from servile obligations and perverse habits, endowed with property, wisdom, and health. Hundreds will expand, with inconceivable rapidity into thousands and thousands, into millions; and a new race, tutored in truth, may, in a few centuries, overflow the habitable world.

Such were the visions of youth! I could not banish them from my mind. I knew them to be crude; but believed that deliberation would bestow upon them solidity and shape. Meanwhile I imparted them to Ludloe.

Chapter VI.

In answer to the reveries and speculations which I sent to him respecting this subject, Ludloe informed me, that they had led his mind into a new sphere of meditation. He had long and deeply considered in what way he might essentially promote my happiness. He had entertained a faint hope that I would one day be qualified for a station like that to which he himself had been advanced. This post required an elevation and stability of views which human beings seldom reach, and which could be attained by me only by a long series of heroic labours. Hitherto every new stage in my intellectual progress had added vigour to his hopes, and he cherished a stronger belief than formerly that my career would terminate auspiciously. This, however, was necessarily distant. Many preliminaries must first be settled; many arduous accomplishments be first obtained; and my virtue be subjected to severe trials. At present it was not in his power to be more explicit; but if my reflections suggested no better plan, he advised me to settle my affairs in Spain, and return to him immediately. My knowledge of this country would be of the highest use, on the supposition of my ultimately arriving at the honours to which he had alluded; and some of these preparatory measures could be taken only with his assistance, and in his company.

This intimation was eagerly obeyed, and, in a short time, I arrived at Dublin. Meanwhile my mind had copious occupation in commenting on my friend's letter. This scheme, whatever it was, seemed to be suggested by my mention of a plan of colonization, and my preference of that mode of producing extensive and permanent effects on the condition of mankind. It was easy therefore to conjecture that this mode had been pursued under some mysterious modifications and conditions.

It had always excited my wonder that so obvious an expedient had been overlooked. The globe which we inhabit was very imperfectly known. The regions and nations unexplored, it was reasonable to believe, surpassed in extent, and perhaps in populousness, those with which we were familiar. The order of Jesuits had furnished an example of all the errors and excellencies of such a scheme. Their plan was founded on erroneous notions of religion and policy, and they had absurdly chosen a scene [*] within reach of the injustice and ambition of an European tyrant.

It was wise and easy to profit by their example. Resting on the two props of fidelity and zeal, an association might exist for ages in the heart of Europe, whose influence might be felt, and might be boundless, in some region of the southern hemisphere; and by whom a moral and political structure might be raised, the growth of pure wisdom, and totally unlike those fragments of Roman and Gothic barbarism, which cover the face of what are called the civilized nations. The belief now rose in my mind that some such scheme had actually been prosecuted, and that Ludloe was a coadjutor. On this supposition, the caution with which he approached to his point, the arduous probation which a candidate for a part on this stage must undergo, and the rigours of that test by which his fortitude and virtue must be tried, were easily explained. I was too deeply imbued with veneration for the effects of such schemes, and too sanguine in my confidence in the rectitude of Ludloe, to refuse my concurrence in any scheme by which my qualifications might at length be raised to a due point.

Our interview was frank and affectionate. I found him situated just as formerly. His aspect, manners, and deportment were the same. I entered once more on my former mode of life, but our intercourse became more frequent. We constantly breakfasted together, and our conversation was usually prolonged through half the morning.

For a time our topics were general. I thought proper to leave to him the introduction of more interesting themes: this, however, he betrayed no inclination to do. His reserve excited some surprise, and I began to suspect that whatever design he had formed with regard to me, had been laid aside. To ascertain this question, I ventured, at length, to recall his attention to the subject of his last letter, and to enquire whether subsequent reflection had made any change in his views.

He said that his views were too momentous to be hastily taken up, or hastily dismissed; the station, my attainment of which depended wholly on myself, was high above vulgar heads, and was to be gained by years of solicitude and labour. This, at least, was true with regard to minds ordinarily constituted; I, perhaps, deserved to be regarded as an exception, and might be able to accomplish in a few months that for which others were obliged to toil during half their lives.

Man, continued he, is the slave of habit. Convince him to-day that his duty leads straight forward: he shall advance, but at every step his belief shall fade; habit will resume its empire, and tomorrow he shall turn back, or betake himself to oblique paths.

We know not our strength till it be tried. Virtue, till confirmed by habit, is a dream. You are a man imbued by errors, and vincible by slight temptations. Deep enquiries must bestow light on your opinions, and the habit of encountering and vanquishing temptation must inspire you with fortitude. Till this be done, you are unqualified for that post, in which you will be invested with divine attributes, and prescribe the condition of a large portion of mankind.

Confide not in the firmness of your principles, or the stedfastness of your integrity. Be always vigilant and fearful. Never think you have enough of knowledge, and let not your caution slumber for a moment, for you know not when danger is near.

I acknowledged the justice of his admonitions, and professed myself willing to undergo any ordeal which reason should prescribe. What, I asked, were the conditions, on the fulfilment of which depended my advancement to the station he alluded to? Was it necessary to conceal from me the nature and obligations of this rank?

These enquiries sunk him more profoundly into meditation than I had ever before witnessed. After a pause, in which some perplexity was visible, he answered:

I scarcely know what to say. As to promises, I claim them not from you. We are now arrived at a point, in which it is necessary to look around with caution, and that consequences should be fully known. A number of persons are leagued together for an end of some moment. To make yourself one of these is submitted to your choice. Among the conditions of their alliance are mutual fidelity and secrecy.

Their existence depends upon this: their existence is known only to themselves. This secrecy must be obtained by all the means which are possible. When I have said thus much, I have informed you, in some degree, of their existence, but you are still ignorant of the purpose contemplated by this association, and of all the members, except myself. So far no dangerous disclosure is yet made: but this degree of concealment is not sufficient. Thus much is made known to you, because it is unavoidable. The individuals which compose this fraternity are not immortal, and the vacancies occasioned by death must be supplied from among the living. The candidate must be instructed and prepared, and they are always at liberty to recede. Their reason must approve the obligations and duties of their station, or they are unfit for it. If they recede, one duty is still incumbent upon them: they must observe an inviolable silence. To this they are not held by any promise. They must weigh consequences, and freely decide; but they must not fail to number among these consequences their own death.

Their death will not be prompted by vengeance. The executioner will say, he that has once revealed the tale is likely to reveal it a second time; and, to prevent this, the betrayer must die. Nor is this the only consequence: to prevent the further revelation, he, to whom the secret was imparted, must likewise perish. He must not console himself with the belief that his trespass will be unknown. The knowledge cannot, by human means, be withheld from this fraternity. Rare, indeed, will it be that his purpose to disclose is not discovered before it can be effected, and the disclosure prevented by his death.

Be well aware of your condition. What I now, or may hereafter mention, mention not again. Admit not even a doubt as to the propriety of hiding it from all the world. There are eyes who will discern this doubt amidst the closest folds of your heart, and your life will instantly be sacrificed.

At present be the subject dismissed. Reflect deeply on the duty which you have already incurred. Think upon your strength of mind, and be careful not to lay yourself under impracticable obligations. It will always be in your power to recede. Even after you are solemnly enrolled a member, you may consult the dictates of your own understanding, and relinquish your post; but while you live, the obligation to be silent will perpetually attend you.

We seek not the misery or death of any one, but we are swayed by an immutable calculation. Death is to be abhorred, but the life of the betrayer is productive of more evil than his death: his death, therefore, we chuse, and our means are instantaneous and unerring.

I love you. The first impulse of my love is to dissuade you from seeking to know more. Your mind will be full of ideas; your hands will be perpetually busy to a purpose into which no human creature, beyond the verge of your brotherhood, must pry. Believe me, who have made the experiment, that compared with this task, the task of inviolable secrecy, all others are easy. To be dumb will not suffice; never to know any remission in your zeal or your watchfulness will not suffice. If the sagacity of others detect your occupations, however strenuously you may labour for concealment, your doom is ratified, as well as that of the wretch whose evil destiny led him to pursue you.

Yet if your fidelity fail not, great will be your recompence. For all your toils and self-devotion, ample will be the retribution. Hitherto you have been wrapt in darkness and storm; then will you be exalted to a pure and unruffled element. It is only for a time that temptation will environ you, and your path will be toilsome. In a few years you will be permitted to withdraw to a land of sages, and the remainder of your life will glide away in the enjoyments of beneficence and wisdom.

Think deeply on what I have said. Investigate your own motives and opinions, and prepare to submit them to the test of numerous hazards and experiments.

Here my friend passed to a new topic. I was desirous of reverting to this subject, and obtaining further information concerning it, but he assiduously repelled all my attempts, and insisted on my bestowing deep and impartial attention on what had already been disclosed. I was not slow to comply with his directions. My mind refused to admit any other theme of contemplation than this.

As yet I had no glimpse of the nature of this fraternity. I was permitted to form conjectures, and previous incidents bestowed but one form upon my thoughts. In reviewing the sentiments and deportment of Ludloe, my belief continually acquired new strength. I even recollected hints and ambiguous allusions in his discourse, which were easily solved, on the supposition of the existence of a new model of society, in some unsuspected corner of the world.

I did not fully perceive the necessity of secrecy; but this necessity perhaps would be rendered apparent, when I should come to know the connection that subsisted between Europe and this imaginary colony. But what was to be done? I was willing to abide by these conditions. My understanding might not approve of all the ends proposed by this fraternity, and I had liberty to withdraw from it, or to refuse to ally myself with them. That the obligation of secrecy should still remain, was unquestionably reasonable.

It appeared to be the plan of Ludloe rather to damp than to stimulate my zeal. He discouraged all attempts to renew the subject in conversation. He dwelt upon the arduousness of the office to which I aspired, the temptations to violate my duty with which I should be continually beset, the inevitable death with which the slightest breach of my engagements would be followed, and the long apprenticeship which it would be necessary for me to serve, before I should be fitted to enter into this conclave.

Sometimes my courage was depressed by these representations. ..... My zeal, however, was sure to revive; and at length Ludloe declared himself willing to assist me in the accomplishment of my wishes. For this end, it was necessary, he said, that I should be informed of a second obligation, which every candidate must assume. Before any one could be deemed qualified, he must be thoroughly known to his associates. For this end, he must determine to disclose every fact in his history, and every secret of his heart. I must begin with making these confessions with regard to my past life, to Ludloe, and must continue to communicate, at stated seasons, every new thought, and every new occurrence, to him. This confidence was to be absolutely limitless: no exceptions were to be admitted, and no reserves to be practised; and the same penalty attended the infraction of this rule as of the former. Means would be employed, by which the slightest deviation, in either case, would be detected, and the deathful consequence would follow with instant and inevitable expedition. If secrecy were difficult to practise, sincerity, in that degree in which it was here demanded, was a task infinitely more arduous, and a period of new deliberation was necessary before I should decide. I was at liberty to pause: nay, the longer was the period of deliberation which I took, the better; but, when I had once entered this path, it was not in my power to recede. After having solemnly avowed my resolution to be thus sincere in my confession, any particle of reserve or duplicity would cost me my life.

This indeed was a subject to be deeply thought upon. Hitherto I had been guilty of concealment with regard to my friend. I had entered into no formal compact, but had been conscious to a kind of tacit obligation to hide no important transaction of my life from him. This consciousness was the source of continual anxiety. I had exerted, on numerous occasions, my bivocal faculty, but, in my intercourse with Ludloe, had suffered not the slightest intimation to escape me with regard to it. This reserve was not easily explained. It was, in a great degree, the product of habit; but I likewise considered that the efficacy of this instrument depended upon its existence being unknown. To confide the secret to one, was to put an end to my privilege: how widely the knowledge would thenceforth be diffused, I had no power to foresee.

Each day multiplied the impediments to confidence. Shame hindered me from acknowledging my past reserves. Ludloe, from the nature of our intercourse, would certainly account my reserve, in this respect, unjustifiable, and to excite his indignation or contempt was an unpleasing undertaking. Now, if I should resolve to persist in my new path, this reserve must be dismissed: I must make him master of a secret which was precious to me beyond all others; by acquainting him with past concealments, I must risk incurring his suspicion and his anger. These reflections were productive of considerable embarrassment.

There was, indeed, an avenue by which to escape these difficulties, if it did not, at the same time, plunge me into greater. My confessions might, in other respects, be unbounded, but my reserves, in this particular, might be continued. Yet should I not expose myself to formidable perils? Would my secret be for ever unsuspected and undiscovered?

When I considered the nature of this faculty, the impossibility of going farther than suspicion, since the agent could be known only by his own confession, and even this confession would not be believed by the greater part of mankind, I was tempted to conceal it.

In most cases, if I had asserted the possession of this power, I should be treated as a liar; it would be considered as an absurd and audacious expedient to free myself from the suspicion of having entered into compact with a daemon, or of being myself an emissary of the grand foe. Here, however, there was no reason to dread a similar imputation, since Ludloe had denied the preternatural pretensions of these airy sounds.

My conduct on this occasion was nowise influenced by the belief of any inherent sanctity in truth. Ludloe had taught me to model myself in this respect entirely with a view to immediate consequences. If my genuine interest, on the whole, was promoted by veracity, it was proper to adhere to it; but, if the result of my investigation were opposite, truth was to be sacrificed without scruple.

* Paraguay.

Chapter VII.

Meanwhile, in a point of so much moment, I was not hasty to determine. My delay seemed to be, by no means, unacceptable to Ludloe, who applauded my discretion, and warned me to be circumspect. My attention was chiefly absorbed by considerations connected with this subject, and little regard was paid to any foreign occupation or amusement.

One evening, after a day spent in my closet, I sought recreation by walking forth. My mind was chiefly occupied by the review of incidents which happened in Spain. I turned my face towards the fields, and recovered not from my reverie, till I had proceeded some miles on the road to Meath. The night had considerably advanced, and the darkness was rendered intense, by the setting of the moon. Being somewhat weary, as well as undetermined in what manner next to proceed, I seated myself on a grassy bank beside the road.

The spot which I had chosen was aloof from passengers, and shrowded in the deepest obscurity.

Some time elapsed, when my attention was excited by the slow approach of an equipage. I presently discovered a coach and six horses, but unattended, except by coachman and postillion, and with no light to guide them on their way. Scarcely had they passed the spot where I rested, when some one leaped from beneath the hedge, and seized the head of the fore-horses. Another called upon the coachman to stop, and threatened him with instant death if he disobeyed. A third drew open the coach-door, and ordered those within to deliver their purses. A shriek of terror showed me that a lady was within, who eagerly consented to preserve her life by the loss of her money.

To walk unarmed in the neighbourhood of Dublin, especially at night, has always been accounted dangerous. I had about me the usual instruments of defence. I was desirous of rescuing this person from the danger which surrounded her, but was somewhat at a loss how to effect my purpose. My single strength was insufficient to contend with three ruffians. After a moment's debate, an expedient was suggested, which I hastened to execute.

Time had not been allowed for the ruffian who stood beside the carriage to receive the plunder, when several voices, loud, clamorous, and eager, were heard in the quarter whence the traveller had come. By trampling with quickness, it was easy to imitate the sound of many feet. The robbers were alarmed, and one called upon another to attend. The sounds increased, and, at the next moment, they betook themselves to flight, but not till a pistol was discharged. Whether it was aimed at the lady in the carriage, or at the coachman, I was not permitted to discover, for the report affrighted the horses, and they set off at full speed.

I could not hope to overtake them: I knew not whither the robbers had fled, and whether, by proceeding, I might not fall into their hands..... These considerations induced me to resume my feet, and retire from the scene as expeditiously as possible. I regained my own habitation without injury.

I have said that I occupied separate apartments from those of Ludloe. To these there were means of access without disturbing the family. I hasted to my chamber, but was considerably surprized to find, on entering my apartment, Ludloe seated at a table, with a lamp before him.

My momentary confusion was greater than his. On discovering who it was, he assumed his accustomed looks, and explained appearances, by saying, that he wished to converse with me on a subject of importance, and had therefore sought me at this secret hour, in my own chamber. Contrary to his expectation, I was absent. Conceiving it possible that I might shortly return, he had waited till now. He took no further notice of my absence, nor manifested any desire to know the cause of it, but proceeded to mention the subject which had brought him hither. These were his words.

You have nothing which the laws permit you to call your own. Justice entitles you to the supply of your physical wants, from those who are able to supply them; but there are few who will acknowledge your claim, or spare an atom of their superfluity to appease your cravings. That which they will not spontaneously give, it is not right to wrest from them by violence. What then is to be done?

Property is necessary to your own subsistence. It is useful, by enabling you to supply the wants of others. To give food, and clothing, and shelter, is to give life, to annihilate temptation, to unshackle virtue, and propagate felicity. How shall property be gained?

You may set your understanding or your hands at work. You may weave stockings, or write poems, and exchange them for money; but these are tardy and meagre schemes. The means are disproportioned to the end, and I will not suffer you to pursue them. My justice will supply your wants.

But dependance on the justice of others is a precarious condition. To be the object is a less ennobling state than to be the bestower of benefit. Doubtless you desire to be vested with competence and riches, and to hold them by virtue of the law, and not at the will of a benefactor...... He paused as if waiting for my assent to his positions. I readily expressed my concurrence, and my desire to pursue any means compatible with honesty. He resumed.

There are various means, besides labour, violence, or fraud. It is right to select the easiest within your reach. It happens that the easiest is at hand. A revenue of some thousands a year, a stately mansion in the city, and another in Kildare, old and faithful domestics, and magnificent furniture, are good things. Will you have them?

A gift like that, replied I, will be attended by momentous conditions. I cannot decide upon its value, until I know these conditions.

The sole condition is your consent to receive them. Not even the airy obligation of gratitude will be created by acceptance. On the contrary, by accepting them, you will confer the highest benefit upon another.

I do not comprehend you. Something surely must be given in return.

Nothing. It may seem strange that, in accepting the absolute controul of so much property, you subject yourself to no conditions; that no claims of gratitude or service will accrue; but the wonder is greater still. The law equitably enough fetters the gift with no restraints, with respect to you that receive it; but not so with regard to the unhappy being who bestows it. That being must part, not only with property but liberty. In accepting the property, you must consent to enjoy the services of the present possessor. They cannot be disjoined.

Of the true nature and extent of the gift, you should be fully apprized. Be aware, therefore, that, together with this property, you will receive absolute power over the liberty and person of the being who now possesses it. That being must become your domestic slave; be governed, in every particular, by your caprice.

Happily for you, though fully invested with this power, the degree and mode in which it will be exercised will depend upon yourself..... You may either totally forbear the exercise, or employ it only for the benefit of your slave. However injurious, therefore, this authority may be to the subject of it, it will, in some sense, only enhance the value of the gift to you.

The attachment and obedience of this being will be chiefly evident in one thing. Its duty will consist in conforming, in every instance, to your will. All the powers of this being are to be devoted to your happiness; but there is one relation between you, which enables you to confer, while exacting, pleasure. .... This relation is *sexual*. Your slave is a woman; and the bond, which transfers her property and person to you, is .... *marriage.*

My knowledge of Ludloe, his principles, and reasonings, ought to have precluded that surprise which I experienced at the conclusion of his discourse. I knew that he regarded the present institution of marriage as a contract of servitude, and the terms of it unequal and unjust. When my surprise had subsided, my thoughts turned upon the nature of his scheme. After a pause of reflection, I answered:

Both law and custom have connected obligations with marriage, which, though heaviest on the female, are not light upon the male. Their weight and extent are not immutable and uniform; they are modified by various incidents, and especially by the mental and personal qualities of the lady.

I am not sure that I should willingly accept the property and person of a woman decrepid with age, and enslaved by perverse habits and evil passions: whereas youth, beauty, and tenderness would be worth accepting, even for their own sake, and disconnected with fortune.

As to altar vows, I believe they will not make me swerve from equity. I shall exact neither service nor affection from my spouse. The value of these, and, indeed, not only the value, but the very existence, of the latter depends upon its spontaneity. A promise to love tends rather to loosen than strengthen the tie.

As to myself, the age of illusion is past. I shall not wed, till I find one whose moral and physical constitution will make personal fidelity easy. I shall judge without mistiness or passion, and habit will come in aid of an enlightened and deliberate choice.

I shall not be fastidious in my choice. I do not expect, and scarcely desire, much intellectual similitude between me and my wife. Our opinions and pursuits cannot be in common. While women are formed by their education, and their education continues in its present state, tender hearts and misguided understandings are all that we can hope to meet with.

What are the character, age, and person of the woman to whom you allude? and what prospect of success would attend my exertions to obtain her favour?

I have told you she is rich. She is a widow, and owes her riches to the liberality of her husband, who was a trader of great opulence, and who died while on a mercantile adventure to Spain. He was not unknown to you. Your letters from Spain often spoke of him. In short, she is the widow of Benington, whom you met at Barcelona. She is still in the prime of life; is not without many feminine attractions; has an ardent and credulent temper; and is particularly given to devotion. This temper it would be easy to regulate according to your pleasure and your interest, and I now submit to you the expediency of an alliance with her.

I am a kinsman, and regarded by her with uncommon deference; and my commendations, therefore, will be of great service to you, and shall be given.

I will deal ingenuously with you. It is proper you should be fully acquainted with the grounds of this proposal. The benefits of rank, and property, and independence, which I have already mentioned as likely to accrue to you from this marriage, are solid and valuable benefits; but these are not the sole advantages, and to benefit you, in these respects, is not my whole view.

No. My treatment of you henceforth will be regulated by one principle. I regard you only as one undergoing a probation or apprenticeship; as subjected to trials of your sincerity and fortitude. The marriage I now propose to you is desirable, because it will make you independent of me. Your poverty might create an unsuitable bias in favour of proposals, one of whose effects would be to set you beyond fortune's reach. That bias will cease, when you cease to be poor and dependent.

Love is the strongest of all human delusions. That fortitude, which is not subdued by the tenderness and blandishments of woman, may be trusted; but no fortitude, which has not undergone that test, will be trusted by us.

This woman is a charming enthusiast. She will never marry but him whom she passionately loves. Her power over the heart that loves her will scarcely have limits. The means of prying into your transactions, of suspecting and sifting your thoughts, which her constant society with you, while sleeping and waking, her zeal and watchfulness for your welfare, and her curiosity, adroitness, and penetration will afford her, are evident. Your danger, therefore, will be imminent. Your fortitude will be obliged to have recourse, not to flight, but to vigilance. Your eye must never close.

Alas! what human magnanimity can stand this test! How can I persuade myself that you will not fail? I waver between hope and fear. Many, it is true, have fallen, and dragged with them the author of their ruin, but some have soared above even these perils and temptations, with their fiery energies unimpaired, and great has been, as great ought to be, their recompence.

But you are doubtless aware of your danger. I need not repeat the consequences of betraying your trust, the rigour of those who will Judge your fault, the unerring and unbounded scrutiny to which your actions, the most secret and indifferent, will be subjected.

Your conduct, however, will be voluntary. At your own option be it, to see or not to see this woman. Circumspection, deliberation forethought, are your sacred duties and highest interest.

Chapter VIII.

Ludloe's remarks on the seductive and bewitching powers of women, on the difficulty of keeping a secret which they wish to know, and to gain which they employ the soft artillery of tears and prayers, and blandishments and menaces, are familiar to all men, but they had little weight with me, because they were unsupported by my own experience. I had never had any intellectual or senti-mental connection with the sex. My meditations and pursuits had all led a different way, and a bias had gradually been given to my feelings, very unfavourable to the refinements of love. I acknowledge, with shame and regret, that I was accustomed to regard the physical and sensual consequences of the sexual relation as realities, and every thing intellectual, disinterested, and heroic, which enthusiasts connect with it as idle dreams. Besides, said I, I am yet a stranger to the secret, on the preservation of which so much stress is laid, and it will be optional with me to receive it or not. If, in the progress of my acquaintance with Mrs. Benington, I should perceive any extraordinary danger in the gift, cannot I refuse, or at least delay to comply with any new conditions from Ludloe? Will not his candour and his affection for me rather commend than disapprove my diffidence? In fine, I resolved to see this lady.

She was, it seems, the widow of Benington, whom I knew in Spain. This man was an English merchant settled at Barcelona, to whom I had been commended by Ludloe's letters, and through whom my pecuniary supplies were furnished....... Much intercourse and some degree of intimacy had taken place between us, and I had gained a pretty accurate knowledge of his character. I had been informed, through different channels, that his wife was much his superior in rank, that she possessed great wealth in her own right, and that some disagreement of temper or views occasioned their separation. She had married him for love, and still doated on him: the occasions for separation having arisen, it seems, not on her side but on his. As his habits of reflection were nowise friendly to religion, and as hers, according to Ludloe, were of the opposite kind, it is possible that some jarring had arisen between them from this source. Indeed, from some casual and broken hints of Benington, especially in the latter part of his life, I had long since gathered this conjecture....... Something, thought I, may be derived from my acquaintance with her husband favourable to my views.

I anxiously waited for an opportunity of acquainting Ludloe with my resolution. On the day of our last conversation, he had made a short excursion from town, intending to return the same evening, but had continued absent for several days. As soon as he came back, I hastened to acquaint him with my wishes.

Have you well considered this matter, said he. Be assured it is of no trivial import. The moment at which you enter the presence of this woman will decide your future destiny. Even putting out of view the subject of our late conversations, the light in which you shall appear to her will greatly influence your happiness, since, though you cannot fail to love her, it is quite uncertain what return she may think proper to make. Much, doubtless, will depend on your own perseverance and address, but you will have many, perhaps insuperable obstacles to encounter on several accounts, and especially in her attachment to the memory of her late husband. As to her devout temper, this is nearly allied to a warm imagination in some other respects, and will operate much more in favour of an ardent and artful lover, than against him.

I still expressed my willingness to try my fortune with her.

Well, said he, I anticipated your consent to my proposal, and the visit I have just made was to her. I thought it best to pave the way, by informing her that I had met with one for whom she had desired me to look out. You must know that her father was one of these singular men who set a value upon things exactly in proportion to the difficulty of obtaining or comprehending them. His passion was for antiques, and his favourite pursuit during a long life was monuments in brass, marble, and parchment, of the remotest antiquity. He was wholly indifferent to the character or conduct of our present sovereign and his ministers, but was extremely solicitous about the name and exploits of a king of Ireland that lived two or three centuries before the flood. He felt no curiosity to know who was the father of his wife's child, but would travel a thousand miles, and consume months, in investigating which son of Noah it was that first landed on the coast of Munster. He would give a hundred guineas from the mint for a piece of old decayed copper no bigger than his nail, provided it had aukward characters upon it, too much defaced to be read. The whole stock of a great bookseller was, in his eyes, a cheap exchange for a shred of parchment, containing half a homily written by St. Patrick. He would have gratefully given all his patrimonial domains to one who should inform him what pendragon or druid it was who set up the first stone on Salisbury plain.

This spirit, as you may readily suppose, being seconded by great wealth and long life, contributed to form a very large collection of venerable lumber, which, though beyond all price to the collector himself, is of no value to his heiress but so far as it is marketable. She designs to bring the whole to auction, but for this purpose a catalogue and description are necessary. Her father trusted to a faithful memory, and to vague and scarcely legible memorandums, and has left a very arduous task to any one who shall be named to the office. It occurred to me, that the best means of promoting your views was to recommend you to this office.

You are not entirely without the antiquarian frenzy yourself. The employment, therefore, will be somewhat agreeable to you for its own sake. It will entitle you to become an inmate of the same house, and thus establish an incessant intercourse between you, and the nature of the business is such, that you may perform it in what time, and with what degree of diligence and accuracy you please.

I ventured to insinuate that, to a woman of rank and family, the character of a hireling was by no means a favourable recommendation.

He answered, that he proposed, by the account he should give of me, to obviate every scruple of that nature. Though my father was no better than a farmer, it is not absolutely certain but that my remoter ancestors had princely blood in their veins: but as long as proofs of my low extraction did not impertinently intrude themselves, my silence, or, at most, equivocal surmises, seasonably made use of, might secure me from all inconveniences on the score of birth. He should represent me, and I was such, as his friend, favourite, and equal, and my passion for antiquities should be my principal inducement to undertake this office, though my poverty would make no objection to a reasonable pecuniary recompense.

Having expressed my acquiescence in his measures, he thus proceeded: My visit was made to my kinswoman, for the purpose, as I just now told you, of paving your way into her family; but, on my arrival at her house, I found nothing but disorder and alarm. Mrs. Benington, it seems, on returning from a longer ride than customary, last Thursday evening, was attacked by robbers. Her attendants related an imperfect tale of somebody advancing at the critical moment to her rescue. It seems, however, they did more harm than good; for the horses took to flight and overturned the carriage, in consequence of which Mrs. Benington was severely bruised. She has kept her bed ever since, and a fever was likely to ensue, which has only left her out of danger to-day.

As the adventure before related, in which I had so much concern, occurred at the time mentioned by Ludloe, and as all other circumstances were alike, I could not doubt that the person whom the exertion of my mysterious powers had relieved was Mrs. Benington: but what an ill-omened interference was mine! The robbers would probably have been satisfied with the few guineas in her purse, and, on receiving these, would have left her to prosecute her journey in peace and security, but, by absurdly offering a succour, which could only operate upon the fears of her assailants, I endangered her life, first by the desperate discharge of a pistol, and next by the fright of the horses........ My anxiety, which would have been less if I had not been, in some degree, myself the author of the evil, was nearly removed by Ludloe's proceeding to assure me that all danger was at an end, and that he left the lady in the road to perfect health. He had seized the earliest opportunity of acquainting her with the purpose of his visit, and had brought back with him her cheerful acceptance of my services. The next week was appointed for my introduction.

With such an object in view, I had little leisure to attend to any indifferent object. My thoughts were continually bent upon the expected introduction, and my impatience and curiosity drew strength, not merely from the character of Mrs. Benington, but from the nature of my new employment. Ludloe had truly observed, that I was infected with somewhat of this antiquarian mania myself, and I now remembered that Benington had frequently alluded to this collection in possession of his wife. My curiosity had then been more than once excited by his representations, and I had formed a vague resolution of making myself acquainted with this lady and her learned treasure, should I ever return to Ireland..... Other incidents had driven this matter from my mind.

Meanwhile, affairs between Ludloe and myself remained stationary. Our conferences, which were regular and daily, related to general topics, and though his instructions were adapted to promote my improvement in the most useful branches of knowledge, they never afforded a glimpse towards that quarter where my curiosity was most active.

The next week now arrived, but Ludloe informed me that the state of Mrs. Benington's health required a short excursion into the country, and that he himself proposed to bear her company. The journey was to last about a fortnight, after which I might prepare myself for an introduction to her.

This was a very unexpected and disagreeable trial to my patience. The interval of solitude that now succeeded would have passed rapidly and pleasantly enough, if an event of so much moment were not in suspense. Books, of which I was passionately fond, would have afforded me delightful and incessant occupation, and Ludloe, by way of reconciling me to unavoidable delays, had given me access to a little closet, in which his rarer and more valuable books were kept.

All my amusements, both by inclination and necessity, were centered in myself and at home. Ludloe appeared to have no visitants, and though frequently abroad, or at least secluded from me, had never proposed my introduction to any of his friends, except Mrs. Benington. My obligations to him were already too great to allow me to lay claim to new favours and indulgences, nor, indeed, was my disposition such as to make society needful to my happiness. My character had been, in some degree, modelled by the faculty which I possessed. This deriving all its supposed value from impenetrable secrecy, and Ludloe's admonitions tending powerfully to impress me with the necessity of wariness and circumspection in my general intercourse with mankind, I had gradually fallen into sedate, reserved, mysterious, and unsociable habits. My heart wanted not a friend.

In this temper of mind, I set myself to examine the novelties which Ludloe's private book-cases contained. 'Twill be strange, thought I, if his favourite volume do not show some marks of my friend's character. To know a man's favourite or most constant studies cannot fail of letting in some little light upon his secret thoughts, and though he would not have given me the reading of these books, if he had thought them capable of unveiling more of his concerns than he wished, yet possibly my ingenuity may go one step farther than he dreams of. You shall judge whether I was right in my conjectures.

Chapter IX.

The books which composed this little library were chiefly the voyages and travels of the missionaries of the sixteenth and seventeenth centuries. Added to these were some works upon political economy and legislation. Those writers who have amused themselves with reducing their ideas to practice, and drawing imaginary pictures of nations or republics, whose manners or government came up to their standard of excellence, were, all of whom I had ever heard, and some I had never heard of before, to be found in this collection. A translation of Aristotle's republic, the political romances of sir Thomas Moore, Harrington, and Hume, appeared to have been much read, and Ludlow had not been sparing of his marginal comments. In these writers he appeared to find nothing but error and absurdity; and his notes were introduced for no other end than to point out groundless principles and false conclusions..... The style of these remarks was already familiar to me. I saw nothing new in them, or different from the strain of those speculations with which Ludlow was accustomed to indulge himself in conversation with me.

After having turned over the leaves of the printed volumes, I at length lighted on a small book of maps, from which, of course, I could reasonably expect no information, on that point about which I was most curious. It was an atlas, in which the maps had been drawn by the pen. None of them contained any thing remarkable, so far as I, who was indeed a smatterer in geography, was able to perceive, till I came to the end, when I noticed a map, whose prototype I was wholly unacquainted with. It was drawn on a pretty large scale, representing two islands, which bore some faint resemblance, in their relative proportions, at least, to Great Britain and Ireland. In shape they were widely different, but as to size there was no scale by which to measure them. From the great number of subdivisions, and from signs, which apparently represented towns and cities, I was allowed to infer, that the country was at least as extensive as the British isles. This map was apparently unfinished, for it had no names inscribed upon it.

I have just said, my geographical knowledge was imperfect. Though I had not enough to draw the outlines of any country by memory, I had still sufficient to recognize what I had before seen, and to discover that none of the larger islands in our globe resembled the one before me. Having such and so strong motives to curiosity, you may easily imagine my sensations on surveying this map. Suspecting, as I did, that many of Ludlow's intimations alluded to a country well known to him, though unknown to others, I was, of course, inclined to suppose that this country was now before me.

In search of some clue to this mystery, I carefully inspected the other maps in this collection. In a map of the eastern hemisphere I soon observed the outlines of islands, which, though on a scale greatly diminished, were plainly similar to that of the land above described.

It is well known that the people of Europe are strangers to very nearly one half of the surface of the globe. [*] From the south pole up to the equator, it is only the small space occupied by southern Africa and by South America with which we are acquainted. There is a vast extent, sufficient to receive a continent as large as North America, which our ignorance has filled only with water. In Ludlow's maps nothing was still to be seen, in these regions, but water, except in that spot where the transverse parallels of the southern tropic and the 150th degree east longitude intersect each other. On this spot were Ludlow's islands placed, though without any name or inscription whatever.

I needed not to be told that this spot had never been explored by any European voyager, who had published his adventures. What authority had Ludlow for fixing a habitable land in this spot? and why did he give us nothing but the courses of shores and rivers, and the scite of towns and villages, without a name?

As soon as Ludlow had set out upon his proposed journey of a fortnight, I unlocked his closet, and continued rummaging among these books and maps till night. By that time I had turned over every book and almost every leaf in this small collection, and did not open the closet again till near the end of that period. Meanwhile I had many reflections upon this remarkable circumstance. Could Ludlow have intended that I should see this atlas? It was the only book that could be styled a manuscript on these shelves, and it was placed beneath several others, in a situation far from being obvious and forward to the eye or the hand. Was it an oversight in him to leave it in my way, or could he have intended to lead my curiosity and knowledge a little farther onward by this accidental disclosure? In either case how was I to regulate my future deportment toward him? Was I to speak and act as if this atlas had escaped my attention or not? I had already, after my first examination of it, placed the volume exactly where I found it. On every supposition I thought this was the safest way, and unlocked the closet a second time, to see that all was precisely in the original order..... How was I dismayed and confounded on inspecting the shelves to perceive that the atlas was gone. This was a theft, which, from the closet being under lock and key, and the key always in my own pocket, and which, from the very nature of the thing stolen, could not be imputed to any of the domestics. After a few moments a suspicion occurred, which was soon changed into certainty by applying to the housekeeper, who told me that Ludlow had returned, apparently in much haste, the evening of the day on which he had set out upon his journey, and just after I had left the house, that he had gone into the room where this closet of books was, and, after a few minutes' stay, came out again and went away. She told me also, that he had made general enquiries after me, to which she had answered, that she had not seen me during the day, and supposed that I had spent the whole of it abroad. From this account it was plain, that Ludlow had returned for no other purpose but to remove this book out of my reach. But if he had a double key to this door, what should hinder his having access, by the same means, to every other locked up place in the house?

This suggestion made me start with terror. Of so obvious a means for possessing a knowledge of every thing under his roof, I had never been till this moment aware. Such is the infatuation which lays our most secret thoughts open to the world's scrutiny. We are frequently in most danger when we deem ourselves most safe, and our fortress is taken sometimes through a point, whose weakness nothing, it should seem, but the blindest stupidity could overlook.

My terrors, indeed, quickly subsided when I came to recollect that there was nothing in any closet or cabinet of mine which could possibly throw light upon subjects which I desired to keep in the dark. The more carefully I inspected my own drawers, and the more I reflected on the character of Ludlow, as I had known it, the less reason did there appear in my suspicions; but I drew a lesson of caution from this circumstance, which contributed to my future safety.

From this incident I could not but infer Ludlow's unwillingness to let me so far into his geographical secret, as well as the certainty of that suspicion, which had very early been suggested to my thoughts, that Ludlow's plans of civilization had been carried into practice in some unvisited corner of the world. It was strange, however, that he should betray himself by such an inadvertency. One who talked so confidently of his own powers, to unveil any secret of mine, and, at the same time, to conceal his own transactions, had surely committed an unpardonable error in leaving this important document in my way. My reverence, indeed, for Ludlow was such, that I sometimes entertained the notion that this seeming oversight was, in truth, a regular contrivance to supply me with a knowledge, of which, when I came maturely to reflect, it was impossible for me to make any ill use. There is no use in relating what would not be believed; and should I publish to the world the existence of islands in the space allotted by Ludlow's maps to these *incognitae*, what would the world answer? That whether the space described was sea or land was of no importance. That the moral and political condition of its inhabitants was the only topic worthy of rational curiosity. Since I had gained no information upon this point; since I had nothing to disclose but vain and fantastic surmises; I might as well be ignorant of every thing. Thus, from secretly condemning Ludlow's imprudence, I gradually passed to admiration of his policy. This discovery had no other effect than to stimulate my curiosity; to keep up my zeal to prosecute the journey I had commenced under his auspices.

I had hitherto formed a resolution to stop where I was in Ludlow's confidence: to wait till the success should be ascertained of my projects with respect to Mrs. Benington, before I made any new advance in the perilous and mysterious road into which he had led my steps. But, before this tedious fortnight had elapsed, I was grown extremely impatient for an interview, and had nearly resolved to undertake whatever obligation he should lay upon me.

This obligation was indeed a heavy one, since it included the confession of my vocal powers. In itself the confession was little. To possess this faculty was neither laudable nor culpable, nor had it been exercised in a way which I should be very much ashamed to acknowledge. It had led me into many insincerities and artifices, which, though not justifiable by any creed, was entitled to some excuse, on the score of youthful ardour and temerity. The true difficulty in the way of these confessions was the not having made them already. Ludlow had long been entitled to this confidence, and, though the existence of this power was venial or wholly innocent, the obstinate concealment of it was a different matter, and would certainly expose me to suspicion and rebuke. But what was the alternative? To conceal it. To incur those dreadful punishments awarded against treason in this particular. Ludlow's menaces still rung in my ears, and appalled my heart. How should I be able to shun them? By concealing from every one what I concealed from him? How was my concealment of such a faculty to be suspected or proved? Unless I betrayed myself, who could betray me?

In this state of mind, I resolved to confess myself to Ludlow in the way that he required, reserving only the secret of this faculty. Awful, indeed, said I, is the crisis of my fate. If Ludlow's declarations are true, a horrid catastrophe awaits me: but as fast as my resolutions were shaken, they were confirmed anew by the recollection—Who can betray me but myself? If I deny, who is there can prove? Suspicion can never light upon the truth. If it does, it can never be converted into certainty. Even my own lips cannot confirm it, since who will believe my testimony?

By such illusions was I fortified in my desperate resolution. Ludlow returned at the time appointed. He informed me that Mrs. Benington expected me next morning. She was ready to depart for her country residence, where she proposed to spend the ensuing summer, and would carry me along with her. In consequence of this arrangement, he said, many months would elapse before he should see me again. You will indeed, continued he, be pretty much shut up from all society. Your books and your new friend will be your chief, if not only companions. Her life is not a social one, because she has formed extravagant notions of the importance of lonely worship and devout solitude. Much of her time will be spent in meditation upon pious books in her closet. Some of it in long solitary rides in her coach, for the sake of exercise. Little will remain for eating and sleeping, so that unless you can prevail upon her to violate her ordinary rules for your sake, you will be left pretty much to yourself. You will have the more time to reflect upon what has hitherto been the theme of our conversations. You can come to town when you want to see me. I shall generally be found in these apartments.

In the present state of my mind, though impatient to see Mrs. Benington, I was still more impatient to remove the veil between Ludlow and myself. After some pause, I ventured to enquire if there was any impediment to my advancement in the road he had already pointed out to my curiosity and ambition.

He replied, with great solemnity, that I was already acquainted with the next step to be taken in this road. If I was prepared to make him my confessor, as to the past, the present, and the future, *without exception or condition*, but what arose from defect of memory, he was willing to receive my confession.

I declared myself ready to do so.

I need not, he returned, remind you of the consequences of concealment or deceit. I have already dwelt upon these consequences. As to the past, you have already told me, perhaps, all that is of any moment to know. It is in relation to the future that caution will be chiefly necessary. Hitherto your actions have been nearly indifferent to the ends of your future existence. Confessions of the past are required, because they are an earnest of the future character and conduct. Have you then—but this is too abrupt. Take an hour to reflect and deliberate. Go by yourself; take yourself to severe task, and make up your mind with a full, entire, and unfailing resolution; for the moment in which you assume this new obligation will make you a new being. Perdition or felicity will hang upon that moment.

This conversation was late in the evening. After I had consented to postpone this subject, we parted, he telling me that he would leave his chamber door open, and as soon as my mind was made up I might come to him.

> * The reader must be reminded that the incidents of this narrative are supposed to have taken place before the voyages of Bougainville and Cook. — Editor.

Chapter X.

I retired accordingly to my apartment, and spent the prescribed hour in anxious and irresolute reflections. They were no other than had hitherto occurred, but they occurred with more force than ever. Some fatal obstinacy, however, got possession of me, and I persisted in the resolution of concealing *one thing*. We become fondly attached to objects and pursuits, frequently for no conceivable reason but the pain and trouble they cost us. In proportion to the danger in which they involve us do we cherish them. Our darling potion is the poison that scorches our vitals.

After some time, I went to Ludloe's apartment. I found him solemn, and yet benign, at my entrance. After intimating my compliance with the terms prescribed, which I did, in spite of all my labour for composure, with accents half faultering, he proceeded to put various questions to me, relative to my early history.

I knew there was no other mode of accomplishing the end in view, but by putting all that was related in the form of answers to questions; and when meditating on the character of Ludloe, I experienced excessive uneasiness as to the consummate art and penetration which his questions would manifest. Conscious of a purpose to conceal, my fancy invested my friend with the robe of a judicial inquisitor, all whose questions should aim at extracting the truth, and entrapping the liar.

In this respect, however, I was wholly disappointed. All his inquiries were general and obvious. — They betokened curiosity, but not suspicion; yet there were moments when I saw, or fancied I saw, some dissatisfaction betrayed in his features; and when I arrived at that period of my story which terminated with my departure, as his companion, for Europe, his pauses were, I thought, a little longer and more museful than I liked. At this period, our first conference ended. After a talk, which had commenced at a late hour, and had continued many hours, it was time to sleep, and it was agreed that next morning the conference should be renewed.

On retiring to my pillow, and reviewing all the circumstances of this interview, my mind was filled with apprehension and disquiet. I seemed to recollect a thousand things, which showed that Ludloe was not fully satisfied with my part in this interview. A strange and nameless mixture of wrath and of pity appeared, on recollection, in the glances which, from time to time, he cast upon me. Some emotion played upon his features, in which, as my fears conceived, there was a tincture of resentment and ferocity. In vain I called my usual sophistries to my aid. In vain I pondered on the inscrutable nature of my peculiar faculty. In vain I endeavoured to persuade myself, that, by telling the truth, instead of entitling myself to Ludloe's approbation, I should only excite his anger, by what he could not but deem an attempt to impose upon his belief an incredible tale of impossible events. I had never heard or read of any instance of this faculty. I supposed the case to be absolutely singular, and I should be no more entitled to credit in proclaiming it, than if I should maintain that a certain billet of wood possessed the faculty of articulate speech. It was now, however, too late to retract. I had been guilty of a solemn and deliberate concealment. I was now in the path in which there was no turning back, and I must go forward.

The return of day's encouraging beams in some degree quieted my nocturnal terrors, and I went, at the appointed hour, to Ludloe's presence. I found him with a much more cheerful aspect than I expected, and began to chide myself, in secret, for the folly of my late apprehensions.

After a little pause, he reminded me, that he was only one among many, engaged in a great and arduous design. As each of us, continued he, is mortal, each of us must, in time, yield his post to another.—Each of us is ambitious to provide himself a successor, to have his place filled by one selected and instructed by himself. All our personal feelings and affections are by no means intended to be swallowed up by a passion for the general interest; when they can be kept alive and be brought into play, in subordination and subservience to the *great end*, they are cherished as useful, and revered as laudable; and whatever austerity and rigour you may impute to my character, there are few more susceptible of personal regards than I am.

You cannot know, till *you* are what *I* am, what deep, what all-absorbing interest I have in the success of my tutorship on this occasion. Most joyfully would I embrace a thousand deaths, rather than that you should prove a recreant. The consequences of any failure in your integrity will, it is true, be fatal to yourself: but there are some minds, of a generous texture, who are more impatient under ills they have inflicted upon others, than of those they have brought upon themselves; who had rather perish, themselves, in infamy, than bring infamy or death upon a benefactor.

Perhaps of such noble materials is your mind composed. If I had not thought so, you would never have been an object of my regard, and therefore, in the motives that shall impel you to fidelity, sincerity, and perseverance, some regard to my happiness and welfare will, no doubt, have place.

And yet I exact nothing from you on this score. If your own safety be insufficient to controul you, you are not fit for us. There is, indeed, abundant need of all possible inducements to make you faithful. The task of concealing nothing from me must be easy. That of concealing every thing from others must be the only arduous one. The *first* you can hardly fail of performing, when the exigence requires it, for what motive can you possibly have to practice evasion or disguise with me? You have surely committed no crime; you have neither robbed, nor murdered, nor betrayed. If you have, there is no room for the fear of punishment or the terror of disgrace to step in, and make you hide your guilt from me. You cannot dread any further disclosure, because I can have no interest in your ruin or your shame: and what evil could ensue the confession of the foulest murder, even before a bench of magistrates, more dreadful than that which will inevitably follow the practice of the least concealment to me, or the least undue disclosure to others?

You cannot easily conceive the emphatical solemnity with which this was spoken. Had he fixed piercing eyes on me while he spoke; had I perceived him watching my looks, and labouring to penetrate my secret thoughts, I should doubtless have been ruined: but he fixed his eyes upon the floor, and no gesture or look indicated the smallest suspicion of my conduct. After some pause, he continued, in a more pathetic tone, while his whole frame seemed to partake of his mental agitation.

I am greatly at a loss by what means to impress you with a full conviction of the truth of what I have just said. Endless are the sophistries by which we seduce ourselves into perilous and doubtful paths. What we do not see, we disbelieve, or we heed not. The sword may descend upon our infatuated head from above, but we who are, meanwhile, busily inspecting the ground at our feet, or gazing at the scene around us, are not aware or apprehensive of its irresistible coming. In this case, it must not be seen before it is felt, or before that time comes when the danger of incurring it is over. I cannot withdraw the veil, and disclose to your view the exterminating angel. All must be vacant and blank, and the danger that stands armed with death at your elbow must continue to be totally invisible, till that moment when its vengeance is provoked or unprovokable. I will do my part to encourage you in good, or intimidate you from evil. I am anxious to set before you all the motives which are fitted to influence your conduct; but how shall I work on your convictions?

Here another pause ensued, which I had not courage enough to interrupt. He presently resumed.

Perhaps you recollect a visit which you paid, on Christmas day, in the year − −, to the cathedral church at Toledo. Do you remember?

A moment's reflection recalled to my mind all the incidents of that day. I had good reason to remember them. I felt no small trepidation when Ludloe referred me to that day, for, at the moment, I was doubtful whether there had not been some bivocal agency exerted On that occasion. Luckily, however, it was almost the only similar occasion in which it had been wholly silent.

I answered in the affirmative. I remember them perfectly.

And yet, said Ludloe, with a smile that seemed intended to disarm this declaration of some of its terrors, I suspect your recollection is not as exact as mine, nor, indeed, your knowledge as extensive. You met there, for the first time, a female, whose nominal uncle, but real father, a dean of that ancient church, resided in a blue stone house, the third from the west angle of the square of St. Jago.

All this was exactly true.

This female, continued he, fell in love with you. Her passion made her deaf to all the dictates of modesty and duty, and she gave you sufficient intimations, in subsequent interviews at the same place, of this passion; which, she being fair and enticing, you were not slow in comprehending and returning. As not only the safety of your intercourse, but even of both your lives, depended on being shielded even from suspicion, the utmost wariness and caution was observed in all your proceedings. Tell me whether you succeeded in your efforts to this end.

I replied, that, at the time, I had no doubt but I had.

And yet, said he, drawing something from his pocket, and putting it into my hand, there is the slip of paper, with the preconcerted emblem inscribed upon it, which the infatuated girl dropped in your sight, one evening, in the left aisle of that church. That paper you imagined you afterwards burnt in your chamber lamp. In pursuance of this token, you deferred your intended visit, and next day the lady was accidentally drowned, in passing a river. Here ended your connexion with her, and with her was buried, as you thought, all memory of this transaction.

I leave you to draw your own inference from this disclosure. Meditate upon it when alone. Recal all the incidents of that drama, and labour to conceive the means by which my sagacity has been able to reach events that took place so far off, and under so deep a covering. If you cannot penetrate these means, learn to reverence my assertions, that I cannot be deceived; and let sincerity be henceforth the rule of your conduct towards me, not merely because it is right, but because concealment is impossible.

We will stop here. There is no haste required of us. Yesterday's discourse will suffice for to-day, and for many days to come. Let what has already taken place be the subject of profound and mature reflection. Review, once more, the incidents of your early life, previous to your introduction to me, and, at our next conference, prepare to supply all those deficiencies occasioned by negligence, forgetfulness, or design on our first. There must be some. There must be many. The whole truth can only be disclosed after numerous and repeated conversations. These must take place at considerable intervals, and when *all* is told, then shall you be ready to encounter the final ordeal, and load yourself with heavy and terrific sanctions.

I shall be the proper judge of the completeness of your confession.—Knowing previously, and by unerring means, your whole history, I shall be able to detect all that is deficient, as well as all that is redundant. Your confessions have hitherto adhered to the truth, but deficient they are, and they must be, for who, at a single trial, can detail the secrets of his life? whose recollection can fully serve him at an instant's notice? who can free himself, by a single effort, from the dominion of fear and shame? We expect no miracles of fortitude and purity from our disciples. It is our discipline, our wariness, our laborious preparation that creates the excellence we have among us. We find it not ready made.

I counsel you to join Mrs. Benington without delay. You may see me when and as often as you please. When it is proper to renew the present topic, it shall be renewed. Till then we will be silent.—Here Ludloe left me alone, but not to indifference or vacuity. Indeed I was overwhelmed with the reflections that arose from this conversation. So, said I, I am still saved, if I have wisdom enough to use the opportunity, from the consequences of past concealments. By a distinction which I had wholly overlooked, but which could not be missed by the sagacity and equity of Ludloe, I have praise for telling the truth, and an excuse for withholding some of the truth. It was, indeed, a praise to which I was entitled, for I have made no *additions* to the tale of my early adventures. I had no motive to exaggerate or dress out in false colours. What I sought to conceal, I was careful to exclude entirely, that a lame or defective narrative might awaken no suspicions.

The allusion to incidents at Toledo confounded and bewildered all my thoughts. I still held the paper he had given me. So far as memory could be trusted, it was the same which, an hour after I had received it, I burnt, as I conceived, with my own hands. How Ludloe came into possession of this paper; how he was apprised of incidents, to which only the female mentioned and myself were privy; which she had too good reason to hide from all the world, and which I had taken infinite pains to bury in oblivion, I vainly endeavoured to conjecture.